"We shouldn't be

"Maybe." He bur
nibbled the soft

He continued to kiss her, nuzzling
to her mouth. Full lips. Soft. Sweet. Just like the woman. He deepened the kiss, waiting for her to open for him.

"Georgie?" He murmured her name against her lips.

She leaned back and stared at him, looking helpless and unsure.

"Sweet pea? What is it?"

"I've wanted this...you... I've dreamed about it...but..."

"Shh, darlin'. This is good. We're good." And it shocked him to realize he spoke the truth. This wasn't a simple seduction. He *liked* Georgie. As a person. And was just now discovering how truly sexy she was. Coming into a relationship from this direction was a revelation. "We're more than good, Georgie."

He recognized her surrender in the way her eyes softened and went unfocused, in the way her arms crept around his neck, in the way her lips sought his and her body pressed against him. "Will you stay with me tonight, Georgie? In my bed?"

* * *

The Boss and His Cowgirl is part of the Red Dirt Royalty series: These Oklahoma millionaires work hard and play harder

Dear Reader,

When I started writing this book, I knew Clay, the oldest Barron brother, had a legacy to fulfill and that his political aspirations defined his life. Georgie, to be his heroine, had to be politically savvy, intelligent and willing to make sacrifices to his career. I didn't know she would be faced with a life-threatening illness and that sacrifice would become a theme of the story.

During the course of writing this book, I lost a friend to breast cancer, learned another was fighting the disease, and a third seems to have conquered it and is living her life to the fullest with her very own real-life hero. These three strong women showed me the way to tell Clay and Georgie's story, and how to give this couple their happy-ever-after.

That's the thing about reading—and writing—romance. There's always a happy ending, even when that ending isn't what we expect it to be.

October is Breast Cancer Awareness month but any time is a good time to get checked. Don't wait until then. Make an appointment while you're thinking about it. Do self-exams and get mammograms. Then go live your life with joy. Love and be loved. Dream. Here's wishing a happy-ever-after to all of you.

I love interacting with readers on my blog, Twitter and Facebook. You can find me at silverjames.com.

Happy reading.

Silver James

SILVER JAMES

THE BOSS AND HIS COWGIRL

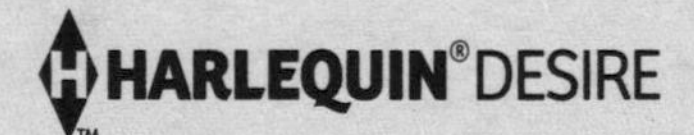

ISBN-13: 978-0-373-73465-8

The Boss and His Cowgirl

This edition published by arrangement with Harlequin Books S.A.

For questions and comments about the quality of this book, please contact us at CustomerService@Harlequin.com.

Printed in U.S.A.

Silver James likes walks on the wild side and coffee. Okay. She LOVES coffee. A cowgirl at heart, she's been an army officer's wife and mom, and worked in the legal field, fire service and law enforcement. Now retired from the real world, she lives in Oklahoma, spending her days writing with the assistance of two Newfoundlands, the cat who rules them all and the characters living in her imagination.

Books by Silver James

Harlequin Desire

Red Dirt Royalty

Cowgirls Don't Cry
The Cowgirl's Little Secret
The Boss and His Cowgirl

Visit her Author Profile page at Harlequin.com, or silverjames.com, for more titles.

To Jenny, Connie, Mac and Warriors
in Pink everywhere.

One

Clayton Barron owned the room—held the emotions, the very hearts and minds of his audience in the palm of his hand. He controlled them with the power of his voice and the words he uttered with such complete conviction. He was in charge, just the way he preferred it. He'd been born, bred and raised to be a US senator—and more. Now into his second term, he stood at the podium of the convention of the Western States Landowners Association in Phoenix, Arizona, and the words rolled off his tongue, his voice infused with sincerity.

Georgeanne Dreyfus, his communications director, had written and fine-tuned the speech. The phrases she'd crafted pushed all the right buttons for this audience. Just as they'd practiced at the hotel last night, he paused for a beat then raised his chin and squared his shoulders.

"I understand your frustration. My great-great-grandfather settled the Crown B Ranch long before Oklahoma achieved statehood. He worked that ranch with his own hands. He survived storms, fires, droughts and floods all so he could leave the land—our birthright—to his children and their children." He inhaled and shifted his expression to reflect a hint of arrogance. "It's time we acknowledge our family legacies. We live on the land. Work it every single day of our lives, from sunrise to dark. It's time we tell the government to back off. It's time they stop tying our hands with their arbitrary rules and regulations. It's time we take back what is ours."

The room erupted into cheers, whistles and loud applause. He basked in the crowd's admiration. After a long standing ovation, the president of the association crossed the stage to shake his hand and thank him. He glanced toward the back of the room. His chief of staff offered a discreet thumbs-up. The head of Clay's personal security team stood nearby, his restless gaze scanning the room. Time to move through the crowd, glad-handing his way to the exit. He had an hour to make it from downtown Phoenix out to Scottsdale for his next engagement, a fund-raising dinner with some of the party's biggest donors.

His gaze strayed to the indistinct figure standing just off stage. Georgie. He didn't have to see her to picture how she looked—straight-cut bangs, her hair scraped back from her face and twisted up in some impossible way, black eyeglass frames dominating her features. He'd overheard more than one reporter comment on her sexy librarian vibe. She'd been there in the backstage shadows the whole time, listening, and more than likely silently mouthing each word as he spoke it. He quirked the corner of his mouth and winked at her. Georgie had been a steady part of his team almost from the beginning. He relied on her to put heart into his words, to spin the press just right. She worked hard for him and he appreciated her efforts. He was lucky to have her at his side.

He cut his eyes toward the back of the auditorium and tilted his head—Georgie's signal to head out. As soon as he descended the steps from the stage, Boone Tate, his chief of staff and cousin, appeared next to him. Clay was a firm believer in keeping it all in the family.

Boone leaned close to whisper in his ear. "Hunt says there's a group of protesters out front. Local cops are handling them but we shouldn't linger too long."

Working a room like this came naturally to Clay. A quick grip of hands, a few brief words, never stopping, always moving toward his goal—the exit. They reached the convention center's lobby a few short minutes later. Outside, an exuberant crowd milled about, waiting for Clay's appearance. A second, more sinister group pushed against a line of local law enforcement officers.

Hunter Tate, chief of security and Boone's older brother,

arrived and steered Clay away from the wide doors. "Taking the back way out. The SUVs and local police backup will meet us at the loading dock." Flanked by the security team and led by the Phoenix Convention Center's security director, they hurried down a side hallway toward the rear of the huge building.

The group hadn't gone twenty feet when the lights went out and sparks lit up the dark. Choking smoke filled the air. The security team switched on flashlights. Hunter grabbed Clay's elbow, urging him forward.

"Wait." Clay stopped dead. "Where's Georgie?"

"On it." One of the plainclothes security guys peeled off and jogged back the way they'd come, his light bouncing in the swirling fog. He called back over his shoulder, "I'll bring her."

A few minutes later they emerged through a metal fire door. A black SUV waited in the alley between buildings. Sharp reports—too close to the sound of gunfire to be ignored—erupted nearby. The security team surrounded Clay and Boone, ran for the vehicle and pushed them into the backseat.

"No!" Clay resisted. "Georgie. We're not leaving without her." More gunshots—or firecrackers; he wasn't sure at this point—went off and then a woman's high-pitched scream scraped his nerves.

"Aw, crap." Hunter surged through the scrum of security surrounding the car, and Clay leaned around Boone to see.

Georgie lay crumpled at the bottom of the steel loading-dock steps. Police scrambled around the corner chasing a group of people wearing Guy Fawkes masks as they ran away. When Hunter grabbed Georgie, she screamed again but he hauled her to her feet and hustled her to the car. Her face was smudged with residue from the oily smoke, and her glasses looked as if they'd been sprayed with black paint. The poor girl couldn't see a thing.

Boone got out of the car but had to shout to be heard over the commotion. "Georgie, it's okay. We've got you." She visibly relaxed at the sound of his voice and let Hunter bundle her into the backseat. Boone dove in behind her as Hunter jumped into the front seat and told the driver to take off.

The SUV accelerated through the alley and they passed the cops, who had taken the protesters to the ground and were handcuffing them. Sirens wailed a shrieking duet with squealing tires as the SUV careened onto the street. Two police cars and a second SUV with Barron Security forces inside formed the motorcade as they raced away.

Georgie was wedged into the middle of the backseat between Boone and Clay, shivering uncontrollably and gulping air. Her hand flailed, found Clay's and latched on. Clay was too furious to speak. Georgie was his employee and she'd been terrorized by those sons of bitches. Her nails bit into his skin but he ignored the sharp prick. Boone removed her glasses and passed them to Hunter to clean while he took out a handkerchief and gently wiped her face. She shuddered and squeezed Clay's hand harder. He squeezed back.

Hunter twisted around in the front seat and handed the glasses back. Clay took them and gently placed them on Georgie's face. She was shaking and didn't speak. With her glasses back in place, she squinted and looked around. Boone's handkerchief was now a dirty gray so Clay retrieved the one from his back pocket and dabbed at the side of her face closest to him. He gave her hand another squeeze.

"Wh-what happened?" Georgie swallowed and Clay's gaze was drawn to her slender throat.

"Sugar, it's okay." Boone leaned in from the opposite side. "You're safe now."

She inhaled and let her breath out slowly, visibly relaxing as she did so. “The lights. And smoke. I…couldn’t see. Did I fall down?” She raised her right leg and stared at her shredded nylon. “The guy with the gun? Did they get him?” She rubbed her left shoulder with her right hand since Clay still held her left.

“Gun?” Hunter’s voice was sharp.

“I thought…” She inhaled and rubbed at her chest as if breathing deeply hurt. Tears glistened on her lashes and she closed her eyes. “Did I hear gunshots?”

Hunter spoke into the high-tech microphone straddling his jawline and listened before saying, “Probably firecrackers. Police didn’t find any weapons.”

Clay continued to wipe the smoke residue off her cheek. When she winced and jerked her head, he realized her face was bruised. “Someone hit you?” His voice was sharp and demanding.

She shook her head then pressed the heel of her free hand against her forehead. “No. I fell. A couple of times, I think. It was…dark. I couldn’t see anything.” Squeezing her eyes shut, she gulped in air.

Clay was afraid she’d hyperventilate. “You’re okay, Georgie. Where else are you hurt?”

Georgie glanced down. Her skirt and jacket were both torn. There were runs in her hose and both knees were scraped and bleeding. Another deep breath had her clutching her side. “Ow.”

“What is it?” Clay didn’t recognize his own voice and regretted sounding so gruff that Georgie jerked away from him. He hadn’t released the hand he held so she didn’t get far.

“I’m sorry.” She turned worried eyes to him then glanced away. “This is my fault. I didn’t mean to make you angry.”

He made an effort to soften his voice. “This isn’t your fault and I’m not angry with you. I’m angry at the protesters. I’m angry because this happened to you, Georgie. Understood?" He smoothed his thumb in small circles against the back of her hand. "We're headed to the hotel so you can get cleaned up. Don't…just don't worry."

Her bottom lip quivered and she closed her eyes again. Clay cut his eyes to Hunter. The other man's expression was remote but for the regret and anger in his eyes.

"My fault. It won't happen again, Senator."

Clay nodded. Working so closely with family could blur the lines but Hunter knew his team had screwed up. He acknowledged it by using Clay's title. From the looks of things as they'd left the alley, the local authorities had the perpetrators in custody. Hunt would make sure the protesters were prosecuted.

As the SUV careened around a corner, Georgie slammed her head back against the seat and groaned. Before Clay could react, Boone had her leaning forward and was gently probing the back of her head.

"Sugar, that's a big lump you've got back there."

"Oh…uh… I think I hit a metal cabinet or something. The first time I fell. As I stood up. Maybe." She settled carefully against the back of the seat.

Boone carried on a quiet conversation over his cell phone, making arrangements for their party to arrive late at the Scottsdale fund-raiser. Without discussing it, Clay decided to leave Georgie at the hotel, along with one of the security team members. The poor girl was obviously upset, not that he blamed her. She was bruised, bloody and probably had injuries she didn't even realize she had.

Driving the wrong way, the convoy pulled into the guest exit of the Barron's Desert Crown Resort in Scottsdale. The security team wanted Clay, who was sitting behind the driver, to exit closest to the hotel's entry. The squad disembarked from their vehicle and formed a phalanx to move Clay through the lobby and onto the elevator. When his door opened, Clay stepped out and pulled Georgie out after him, refusing to relinquish her hand. He felt connected to her and protective.

A barrage of camera flashes flared and Georgie stumbled. Without thinking, Clay swept her into his arms in a princess carry. Her arms circled his neck and she buried her face against his shoulder, hiding from the cameras and shouted questions. His anger surged again but cooler heads prevailed as Boone and Hunter guided him through the lobby and onto a waiting elevator, ignoring the reporters yelling for a statement.

The express ride took them straight to the penthouse level where Clay occupied the Sonoma Suite, the hotel's equivalent of presidential lodging. He met Boone's surprised expression with quiet directions. "Go to her room and get her bags. She'll stay up here in the empty guest room."

Comprised of a living room, formal dining room, study, kitchen facilities and four bedrooms with attached baths, there was room for Clay, Boone, Hunter and now Georgie. He didn't want her alone in some random hotel room, even though every room in his family's resort was five-star. He wanted her safe and he wasn't convinced she would be out of his sight—irrational as that sounded. Without breaking stride, Clay continued into the master bedroom and straight to the massive bath. He set her on the marble vanity top without regard to the gray smudges smeared across his white Western-cut shirt. He almost smiled at the impression his turquoise bolo tie had left on Georgie's cheek. Keeping a hand on her shoulder to hold her steady, he grabbed a washcloth and wet it, squeezing out the excess water with one hand.

She remained bug-eyed, her pupils dilated, and he could almost feel her shock. Her hair, normally in a neat bun at the back of her head, was tousled and framing her pale face—and was far longer than he'd realized. With gentleness he didn't know he possessed, Clay removed her glasses and set them in the sink to be washed. He wiped her face first, rinsing the cloth before moving to her skinned knees. Her hands, clenched into tight balls on her lap, slowly relaxed.

He'd never been this…intimate with her before. They worked closely together but touching her like this? She was…Georgie. Always there when he needed a press release, a statement or a sounding board. She was efficient. Professional. And he was surprised at the curves he'd discovered when he picked her up. He realized, belatedly, that there was a very feminine woman lurking beneath her rather dowdy exterior.

Then he remembered why she was sitting on the counter in his bathroom. Anger flashed through him as hot as a grease fire. "Dammit, Georgie. This shouldn't have happened. Especially not to you."

She blinked, squinted, did her best to focus her eyes on his face. "Yeah, well." She lifted one shoulder in a shrug.

"Boone's gone to your room to get your things. Stay in here and get cleaned up. Then I want you to move into the other guest room." He tilted his head toward the door. "There's a robe on the back of the door. Okay?"

She fumbled for her glasses. He snatched them first, washed and dried them before handing them to her. Once they were back on her face, she looked more like herself, and her green eyes lost some of that shell-shocked glaze. Her nose wrinkled as she sniffed her shoulder. "Yeah, I definitely want out of these clothes. They stink like smoke."

Clay backed away. "I'll get out of here so you have some privacy."

She nodded but didn't speak so he gave her arm a little pat and steadied her as she slipped off the counter to stand on the marble floor. Once she had her balance, he backed out of the room, shutting the door firmly behind him. He almost ran over Hunter, who'd been hovering just outside.

"Dammit, Hunt. How did this happen? How did the protesters get inside?" Clay was as angry at himself as he was his security chief. Security should have watched out for her. Hell, *he* should have watched out for her. She was, ultimately, his responsibility.

Hunt made a noise that resembled a growl. "A group came through a secondary entrance in the basement and got to the main control board. Building security thinks it might have been an inside job. They're investigating."

Lightning flashed beyond the sheer curtains covering the bedroom window, followed shortly by thunder. Frowning, Hunt pulled out his cell phone, swiped the screen then punched an app icon. "I didn't know we had weather moving in tonight." He checked the forecast and radar then shrugged. "Nothing but boomers and some rain. Now, about Georgie. It won't happen again, Clay. I promise. I'll put a man on her personally."

Clay tunneled his fingers through his hair. "As soon as she's—" A massive boom rattled the window glass and seconds later, all the lights in the suite went out. A scream from inside the bathroom had both men scrambling—Hunt for light, Clay for the door handle.

Jerking the door open, Clay found Georgie kneeling on the floor, her head down, shoulders hunched. Was she gagging? Jeez, but he hated that sound. Had ever since college and drunken frat parties. He kicked the door shut in Hunter's face and bent down. Using the flashlight app on his cell, he checked her over. Clay lifted her long brown hair back from her face, though she tried to turn away. Georgie's throat worked as she swallowed hard, coughing with the effort.

To combat his very visceral reaction to what was happening, Clay recited the Gettysburg Address. Then the Preamble to the US Constitution. He figured he'd have to start on the Declaration of Independence next but Georgie finally inhaled and turned an apologetic gaze on him. He stood to retrieve another washcloth.

"I'm sorry," she murmured, not looking at him as he crouched beside her.

He wondered if her heightened color was a result of exertion or embarrassment. "It's okay—" He bit off the next word, an endearment that slipped too easily into his head. To cover, he brushed her hair back over her shoulders. Pet names didn't come as easy to him as they did Boone. The fact that one had formed on his tongue should have concerned him, but he couldn't work up the energy to worry about it at the moment. He handed her the washcloth and she wiped her mouth and face but still wouldn't look at him. It was then he realized she'd stripped down to a bra and panties—red ones. He refused to process that visual, focusing instead on the situation. "What happened? You seemed okay when I walked out."

Georgie swallowed a dry heave and wrapped her arms around her chest. "I…panicked. The dark. And the storm. I'm a tad…claustrophobic. Or something."

Clay swallowed the insane urge to laugh as his adrenaline rush faded. He bit the insides of his cheeks and when that didn't help, he bit his tongue in an aborted effort to stop the sputtering laugh that finally escaped. He immediately apologized. "It's not funny. I know. I'm sorry."

A choking sound spurted from her. She'd hidden her face in her hands so he snagged the robe from the back of the door and draped it across her shoulders and back. She slipped her arms into the sleeves and twisted her body so she could see him. Clay was surprised to see her biting her lips as if she, too, was trying to hold back her laughter. Then the robe gapped and he glimpsed the bruise on her ribs. He curled his hands into fists to keep from ripping the robe off to examine her. Those bastards had marked her with their idiotic stunt. That quelled his urge to laugh.

"You're bruised, Georgie. And you have that bump on your head. I'd like a doctor to look at you, okay?"

Her forehead furrowed in confusion before she glanced down and saw what he was talking about. "Oh. I am. Huh." Her gaze caught on his. "I was too busy being scared witless to notice, and it was dark so I couldn't see…"

She rubbed absently at her pale skin, and Clay reminded himself Georgie was in his employ and traumatized. He was not as big a jerk as his father or brothers when it came to women. He refused to be, but damn if he wasn't suddenly aware that Georgie had been hiding some very interesting attributes behind her boxy suits and thick glasses—said attributes all but staring him in the face, despite the modest cut of that red lingerie and the robe.

"I'll have the house doctor check you once the electricity—" The lights flickered, steadied and remained on. "Speaking of. Ready to get into the shower now?"

Clay stood and extended his hand to help her up. Just as she clasped his fingers, another clap of thunder shook the building and the lights extinguished. He felt her tremble and hunkered down beside her once more. "It's okay, Georgie."

He swiped his phone and when the screen lit up, he tapped the flashlight app once more. "See? We have light."

Georgie was panting again and a thin sheen of perspiration covered her face. "I'm sorry. This is stupid. I know it's stupid and irrational."

"Fear is—" The light on his phone dimmed and he glanced at the battery indicator. He flicked off the flashlight app, but the home-screen light cast a soft glow over Georgie's face. "Sorry. I'm down to the dregs of battery life. We can go outside, into the bedroom."

"No. There might be monsters under the bed."

Clay studied her face in the ghostly glow of his cell. A hint of a smile tweaked her lips. Good. This was the Georgie he knew and…liked. Yes, definitely liked. He liked

Georgie. She was his employee. He was only keeping her company in his bathroom because she'd had a traumatic day.

"I promise to slay the monsters."

"Or legislate them out of existence?"

"I can do that. I'll introduce a bill in the Senate. And then I'll take you dancing in the dark."

"Isn't that a song?"

"Springsteen."

She blinked at him, her eyes owlish behind the lenses of her glasses. "You're a fan of the Boss?"

"Hey, just because I grew up on Waylon, Willie and the boys, doesn't mean I don't have refined tastes in music."

That elicited a giggle. "Are you trying to distract me?"

"Depends. Is it working?"

"Sort of."

"Then yes." He eased down to the floor, stretching his legs out. "I'm going to take a shot in the dark here—"

"Peter Sellers!"

"I'm sorry. You didn't phrase that in the form of question." He winked at her.

"Oh, getting technical, are we? Fine. I'll take Dark for three hundred, Alex."

"Hmm. Okay." The light from his phone blinked out. Clay didn't like Georgie's quick inhalation. He tapped the phone, thinking it had just gone into sleep mode. Nothing happened. "Sorry, Georgie. I think the battery died."

"O-okay. Um…can we keep playing?"

"Sure. Dark for three hundred, right?"

"Yes."

"Ha! Got one. Michelle Pfeiffer plays the family matriarch in this—"

"What is *Dark Shadows*?"

Georgie laughed as he huffed in pretended frustration. "How did you know that?"

"Clay, your crush on Michelle Pfeiffer is not exactly a secret around the office."

"It isn't?" He did his best to sound both shocked and innocent, but damn if he didn't like the sound of his name coming from between her lips. He couldn't remember if she'd ever called him by his first name—at least not up close and personal like this.

"I'll take Dark for a thousand, Alex."

He racked his brain for an answer and when it came to him, he grinned. "Come to the dark side. We have cookies."

A sound that was a cross bctwccn a gigglc and snort erupted from Georgie. "How do you even know that?"

The next thing Clay knew, Georgie was laughing—a deep belly laugh that almost lit up the dark with its happy sound. And just like that, the lights blazed, chasing the shadows away. As she dissolved into more laughter, relieved this time, he joined her. This was a side of Georgie he appreciated—her irreverent sense of humor. Working, she was reserved, thoughtful, erudite. She had a way of boiling down an issue into sound bites. She was knowledgeable and intelligent and he thought of her as his personal… His thoughts trailed off as he stared into her eyes—eyes a shade of green he was currently trying, and failing, to describe.

With a start, he realized Georgie was no longer laughing. She'd devolved into hiccuping sobs. He hated tears. The women his father married too often resorted to them, but Georgie's were real and earned. He gathered her close, stroking his palm down her back in long caresses.

"You're okay, Georgie. You're safe."

She nodded, fighting for control. "I know. I'm…" She sniffed, looked around for a tissue, then gave up and wiped her nose on the sleeve of her robe. "Sorry, boss. I'm okay. Just…nerves. I hate the dark. Hate small spaces, especially in the dark."

"Want to tell me?"

She shook her head but words tumbled out. “I was a kid. Got trapped in our old storm cellar. In the dark. Took my folks a couple of hours to find me.”

He tightened his arm around her and fought the urge to kiss the top of her head. “Yeah, that would not be fun.”

Georgie snuffled again so Clay reached for the roll of toilet paper and ripped off a strip. She took it and tried to discreetly wipe, then blow, her nose. Once she appeared composed, he disengaged and stood. “Why don’t you stay in tonight, Georgie? You deserve a night off.” When she nodded, he opened the door and edged toward it. “I’ll get out so you can shower.”

She nodded so he helped her up, made sure she was steady and once again retreated. He listened at the door until he heard the shower and then met Boone and Hunt in the living area of the suite. He gave his orders, grabbed clean clothes from his room and ducked into Boone’s room to clean up.

Georgie was still in his bathroom when he was ready to leave for the donor dinner. Part of him wanted to stay, but the practical part, the politician he’d been born, bred and raised to be, marched out of the suite led by his chief of security and trailed by his chief of staff. Georgie would be fine. She had to be. He didn’t stop to contemplate why that mattered so much.

Two

Georgie waited in the master bath huddled in her borrowed robe until all sounds diminished outside. She didn't know what to do about her ruined clothes. Wrinkling her nose didn't help dissipate the smell of smoke. She blamed her reaction on the Phobia Twins—Nycto and Claustro. When the lights had gone out in the already shadowy backstage area, she'd panicked. Like an idiot.

When the security guard found her, she'd screamed like the blonde cheerleader in a teen horror movie. She'd lost count of the times she'd fallen and scraped herself up before he arrived. Then there was that whole thing on the loading dock, in the SUV and at the hotel entrance when— She cut that thought off.

She wanted to bang her head on the nearest hard surface. Her nerves and emotions were caused by fear. Not Clay Barron holding her hand. Or carrying her. Or…nope. Clothes. She had to deal with her clothes because they reeked of smoke and stink bombs.

Checking the trash can, she found an extra folded plastic sack. She mashed the clothes into a ball and stuffed them into the bag, spinning it and tying it off. She shoved the whole thing into the trash. Georgie briefly considered digging out her bottle of spray cologne and using it to drown the odor still lingering. Considering this was Clay's bathroom, that probably wasn't a good idea. Then she thought about using his cologne—the signature scent of almond, cedar, bergamot and lemon that never failed to weaken her knees. Nope. That would not be a smart move, either.

She slipped out of the bathroom, pausing at the master bedroom door to listen. A sports program droned on the big screen TV in the living area and she saw shoulders and a head silhouetted over the back of the couch. Her embarrassment sent her scurrying, but she stopped when the guy spoke.

"You all right, Miss Dreyfus?"

"Y-yes." She didn't recognize the voice and the man didn't turn around, for which she was grateful.

"The senator and his party went to the fund-raiser. Their return ETA is midnight. Mr. Tate moved your things into the guest room next to his on the far side of the suite." He lifted his hand and gestured before continuing. "If you're hungry, I'll order room service. If there's anything else you need, just let me know. I'm Glen."

She clutched the lapels of her robe closer to her chest. Food was the last thing she wanted but she desperately wanted a Diet Coke. "Hi, Glen. Is there… I saw a kitchen. A Diet Coke, maybe?"

"I'll have one sent up, miss."

"Thanks. I'll just be in my…room."

She dashed across the open space and ducked into the bedroom the guard had pointed out. A lamp glowed next to the bed, on which the linens had been turned down. Her suitcase occupied a low bench. Checking the closet, she found her hang-up bag with her clothing inside. The case holding her personal care items had been tucked into the adjoining bath. While not nearly as opulent as the one in the master suite, it was far fancier than the bath in her previous room and was *Architectural Digest*-worthy compared to the one in her apartment back in DC. The room itself, even though it was probably the smallest bedroom in the suite, was magnificent. She needed to focus on something normal—as if brocade coverlets, silken accent rugs and needlepoint chair upholstery was normal. A hysterical giggle erupted from the back of her throat before she could stop it.

Digging through her suitcase, Georgie found her comfort

jammies—worn sweats and a long-sleeved T-shirt that said "Ways to win my heart…1. Buy me coffee 2. Make me coffee 3. Be coffee." Not that she was a caffeine addict. Much. She wondered if there was a coffeemaker in the kitchen. If she couldn't sleep—and she suspected it would be hard—she'd go look. Coffee would be a godsend.

A light tap on the bedroom door had her scrambling back into the robe. "Yes?"

"I've got your Coke, and the hotel doctor is here to see you."

"Doctor?" She'd forgotten, in the midst of her mortification, that Clay had offered to send a doctor. Georgie opened the door a crack and a kindly face with wild black eyebrows peered at her over Glen's shoulder. "Miss Dreyfus, I'm Dr. Bruce. The senator asked me to look in on you."

"Um…sure. Come in." Glen handed her a bottle of Diet Coke so cold it still had little bits of ice clinging to it.

"I'll be right out here, ma'am."

Ma'am? Ouch. She was only thirty. She pushed her glasses to the bridge of her nose and nodded, suddenly reminded of her dowdy looks. Stepping back, she opened the door wide enough for the doctor to enter.

He waved her toward the edge of the bed. "Do you mind sitting here, Ms. Dreyfus? I fear I'll need to do some prodding and poking. I hear you've had quite a day."

The snort escaped before she could stop it. "You could say that."

"Are you wearing anything under the T-shirt? Perhaps a tank or bra?"

Georgie blushed. "Oh, yeah. That would probably keep both of us from being embarrassed. Just a sec." She grabbed a spaghetti-strapped tank and dashed into the bathroom. She whipped off her sweatshirt and pulled the tank on before returning and settling on the bed once again.

She had to lift the tank so he could see her torso. Dr.

Bruce *tsked* at the bruises staining the ribs on her right side and her cheek. He *hmmed* at the knot on the back of her head. "You've got quite a collection of injuries, young lady. Are you in discomfort?"

"Only when I laugh?" She waggled her brows and the man smiled.

"Good to have a sense of humor, Ms. Dreyfus." He made sure her eyes were equal and reactive then checked her blood pressure, temperature and other vital signs before continuing. "You were lucky. You'll be sore for a few days, but the bruises will fade in a week or so." He coiled his stethoscope and dropped it into his bag before digging around in a side pocket. He pulled out a white envelope and wrote on it before retrieving a bottle of pills. He emptied six into the envelope and handed it to her. "I don't see signs of a concussion so I'm prescribing a light sleep aid. I suggest you take two tonight and then use the others as needed. Take one at bedtime over the next few nights. I'll also leave you some cold packs to help with the bruising and the bump. Once you get back to Washington, I want you to see your regular physician if you continue having trouble. Any questions?"

"No, sir. I'm good."

He patted her on the shoulder. "Get some rest, Ms. Dreyfus. That's the best thing for you."

The doctor opened the door and Glen almost fell through. Her guard was taking his duties seriously. He ushered Dr. Bruce out, shutting the door behind him. Georgie looked at the envelope and debated the pros and cons. She hated taking medicine but suspected the doctor was right. She'd replay the day's events—especially Clay's actions—on an endless loop guaranteed to keep her tossing and turning all night. Clay. She had to stop thinking of him by his first name. The senator. Her boss. The unattainable symbol of every feminine fantasy she'd had since the day she'd first walked into his campaign headquarters ten years before.

"Argh!" If her head wasn't already pounding, she might beat it against the wall. "Georgeanne Ruth Dreyfus, you are a complete and utter idiot." In self-defense, she shook two pills into her palm, twisted the top off the Diet Coke and took her medicine. Settling in bed, she snuggled into a world-class pillow.

The song "Girls Just Want to Have Fun" invaded her dream. Over and over. Georgie fumbled for her cell phone but it wasn't on the bedside table. The song stopped and she snuggled back under the covers, her brain as foggy as San Francisco Bay. She'd barely closed her eyes when the song played again. This time she threw off the covers and went hunting. She found the blasted phone in the side pocket of her messenger bag—the bag with the strap that broke yesterday when she tumbled off the loading dock, but was now perfect.

The hair prickled on the back of her neck. She didn't remember bringing it from the car last night and there was no way it could have been repaired. The phone stopped ringing, again, and she noticed the price tag still attached to the intact shoulder strap. This wasn't her bag, even though it was full of her stuff. Hers was a cheap knockoff. This one was the real deal, according to the amount listed on the tag.

Before her brain could cycle through the implications, the phone sang a third time. She answered with a snarled, "What!"

"OMG, Georgie! Are you okay? I've been so worried and then you didn't answer and where are you and are you all right, what happened—" Jennifer Antonelli, her best friend, paused to inhale.

"Slow down, Jen. How did you know something happened?"

"How did I know?" Jen's voice rose in pitch. "How did I know? Georgeanne, you're all over the morning news!"

Her stomach dropped. She found the remote control for the television and thumbed it to life. Scrolling through, she found an all-news channel. And sank to the edge of the bed, her legs no longer steady. "Oh, no. The cameras. I'm screwed."

"Georgie! What the heck happened yesterday? And were you really rescued by the senator?"

She had to put her head between her knees and breathe to keep from hyperventilating and passing out. "Dang, dang, dang," was all she could manage.

Jennifer had no such handicap. "What did it feel like? Is he as strong as he looks? I mean, gracious! He scooped you up and carried you away like…like…I don't know who! Holy cannoli, girl. Clay Barron was like Kevin Costner in that movie where he rescued Whitney Houston. Georgie? Georgie, are you listening to me?"

"Shush, Jen. I'm trying to hear the commentary on TV."

Voices droned in the background as footage played of the Tate brothers hustling her—clothes torn, knees bloody—into the rear seat of the senator's SUV. Clay looked shocked and angry as he ducked back inside to make room for her. The scene changed to their arrival at the hotel. The guards jogged up and opened the back door. Clay emerged holding her hand. Holding her hand? Georgie couldn't breathe for a minute and then, moments later when she stumbled and he swept her into his arms, she choked.

"Oh, God." Panting, she resumed her head-between-knees position.

"Georgie? Georgeanne! Speak to me. Are you okay?"

"No. I need to die. Like right now. No. I would have been better off dying last night. Oh, Mother Goose, Jen. I am *so* screwed."

"You keep saying that! What happened? Have you been holding out on me?"

"No. Oh, dang it, dang it, dang it." Georgie needed coffee. Stat. There was still liquid left in her Diet Coke bottle. She gulped it down and glanced at the clock. Five-fifteen. Arizona didn't do Daylight Savings Time so it was just after 7:00 a.m. in Washington. She rubbed her face and eyes. This was bad. *Really* bad. How many times had she dreamed of a romantic interlude with the senator? Way too often, but never played out in front of cameras. And reporters. On the national news.

Memories crowded in and she swayed. "He saw me, Jen," she whispered into the phone.

"Saw you? What do you mean?"

"In my bra and panties. I…I panicked. He… I think he held me in his lap." In full panic mode, she fled her bedroom, praying there would be a coffeemaker in the kitchen. And stationery. So she could write out her resignation letter. How in the world was she going to face Clay this morning? Sprinting through the living area, she barely noticed the bodyguard jumping to his feet. She sort of waved him back to his chair with a vague motion of her hand.

"Oh, thank you, thank you," she murmured when she spotted a Keurig machine and a display of K-Cups. "Coffee, Jen. Coffee first."

"You okay, Miss Dreyfus?" The guard watched her warily from just beyond the granite bar separating the kitchen from the dining area.

"Yeah. Yes. Coffee. I just need coffee. Sorry to have disturbed you. Um…carry on." She wanted to head-slap herself. Carry on? Seriously? Her foot tapped a jittery rhythm as the machine performed its magic. Once she had a fresh-brewed latte in her hands she could breathe again. Almost. She drained the cup in a few gulps and brewed another.

"Who are you talking to and I'm still waiting for an explanation, missy," Jen hissed through her phone.

"Shhh. I have to get back to my room."

"Back to your room? Where are you?"

"I'm in the senator's suite."

Ducking her head, she dashed back to her room and shut the door, ignoring the guard's grin as she ran past him. "Okay. I can think now. Maybe."

"How in blue blazes did the senator see you in your underwear and please tell me it was the nice stuff and not the ratty granny panties you normally wear!"

"The protesters yesterday. There were smoke bombs. And…they cut the lights, Jen. I was backstage. I fell and banged my head. Tripped on the darn stairs and fell again."

"Jiminy, girl! Are you okay?"

"I have some wicked bruises." She touched the back of her head. The lump remained but wasn't as tender. "And thank goodness, I have a hard head."

Jen's voice turned sly. "Did the senator kiss all your owies to make them better?"

"Jennifer Marie Antonelli, he did not!" Casting a worried glance at her closed door, Georgie lowered her voice. "It wasn't like that. He was holding my hand because he was being nice. And then I tripped getting out of the car because all the camera flashes blinded me. My glasses were smeary and you know how blind I am so—"

"And the man picked you up like you were a fairy-tale princess and carried you off to his castle."

"Well…sort of. They're worried about security because of the protesters so I was moved into his suite. There's lots of room. I mean serious room. Four bedrooms, five baths, all the amenities."

"You're stalling, Georgie. I don't want a travelogue. I want the down and dirty."

She inhaled and blew her breath out through puffed cheeks and pursed lips. In a resigned voice, Georgie recounted the events, ending with, "Then he left."

"Wait. You played strip Jeopardy?"

"My boss saw me in my undies and you're making up games? And what part of him holding me and…and…" She started to hyperventilate again. "OMG, Jen. I have to resign. I can't face the man."

"Breathe, Georgie. Does he have any idea how you feel?"

"You mean have I told him that I love him like crazy and have since the moment I met him? Oh, yeah, right. I definitely confessed that to him last night."

"Your sarcasm is showing. That's a good thing. It means you'll be okay. But you can't quit, Georgie. You have your dream job. Besides, if the man can't look beyond your tighty-whities and see what a jewel you are, he doesn't deserve you."

"Awww, Jen. Loyal to a fault. But they were red."

"I'm serious. You're just panicky. How many times have you had to put your head between your knees this morning?"

Laughter burst from Georgie's mouth. "Too many."

"See? I know you. Now, grab a shower. I'd tell you to put on something sexy but you don't own…wait! Red? You own red panties?"

"And a red bra."

"Are they lacy?"

"Well…um…no."

"Just as I thought. Now go put on your business suit of armor, get more coffee and do what you do best—work. Okay?"

Georgie nodded then remembered Jen couldn't see her. "Okay. You're right."

"Of course I am. I'm always right. I'm your BFF. Keep me posted. I never want to find out stuff like this from the news ever again. *Capisce*?"

"*Capisce*."

Three

Clay stared at the press briefing folder lying front and center on his desk. He did not want to open it. He'd already seen the news coverage of yesterday's fiasco. The file would hold hard copies of clippings and photographs from print media and the internet. Georgie would have put together a digital file of clips, too, and emailed it, but she knew his preference for paper. He leaned back in his chair and swiveled so he could look out the window. A few of the more lurid headlines made him roll his eyes.

Senator Protects Aide à la *The Bodyguard*
Barron Rescues Damsel in Distress
Senator Barron—Hero in Disguise

All the articles led with a photograph of him sweeping Georgie into his arms to carry her. He leaned forward, tapping two fingers on the photo. Georgie must have been up before the Arizona sunrise to cull all the stories from the New York shows and national press and prepare them, though she evidently had gone back to bed. She'd been asleep when he returned from the fund-raising dinner last night. The night guard said she'd taken some prescribed sleeping pills and went right to bed. Her door wasn't locked so Clay had peeked in first thing this morning and she'd been curled up in a semi-fetal position under a thick pile of bedcovers. Then he'd walked into the suite's study and found his desk set up just like every other working day.

Boone rapped his knuckles against the door and sauntered in, leaning a shoulder against the doorjamb. He inclined his head toward the open file. "You've seen the headlines."

Nodding, Clay shuffled through the file, barely glancing at the various photos and clippings. "And the coverage on all the news channels. Your take?"

"You should have a nice bump in the next poll, especially in that all-important women's vote. They'll see you as heroic and dashing now. Let's face it, you're already the most eligible bachelor inside or outside the Beltway, and we all know you've got the Barron good looks." He chuckled. "Tates are more handsome, but you Barrons aren't bad."

Boone reflexively caught the pen Clay tossed at him then sobered. "In all seriousness, now you have that intangible mystique that will draw women. I'm sorry Georgie got caught in the middle, but those protesters did you a huge favor."

Clay growled under his breath. He, too, hated what had happened to Georgie. Her tears just about undid him. He couldn't deal with tears. Hadn't since— He cut off that thought, only to have it replaced by the memory of cradling Georgie in his arms—with very little between them. He'd wanted to take care of her. And maybe a little more. Doing so would have been taking advantage of a bad situation. He was not his father or his younger brothers. He could keep his libido in check.

The curves he discovered when he'd held her had been a surprise, and seeing her in that cute, if rather prim, red lingerie left no doubts. He halted that train of thought and reminded himself that Georgie was...Georgie. She dealt with the press, wrote his speeches and corralled a large portion of his staff. Boone was his right hand and she might as well be his left. Clay kept reminding himself of that. She was his employee, even if thoughts of her made him shift in his desk chair looking for a more comfortable position. Unlike his father, he didn't dip his pen in company ink.

"Is she still asleep?" Clay needed to see her, talk to her.

"Don't think so, but she's not coming out of her room."

"Have you spoken to her?"

"No."

Was Boone fidgeting? "Spit it out, cuz."

Boone stepped fully into the study and closed the door before dropping into a side chair. He put on what Clay called his "headmaster" face before asking, "What happened last night?"

"Happened?"

"Yeah. What went on between you and Georgie while I was packing up her stuff and replacing what had been ruined?"

"That's none of your business, Boone."

"It is if it affects the operation of your office. The two of you spent a lot of time in the bathroom. Alone. With the door shut."

Leaning back in the chair, Clay studied the man he trusted maybe even more than his own brothers. He weighed the pros and cons of disclosure and finally told Boone about their encounter in the bathroom.

"Ah…okay. Yeah. I can see why she's avoiding us this morning, especially given the publicity. Speaking of which, what in the world possessed you to pick her up?"

That was one question Clay hadn't asked himself. "I was right there. It just seemed…prudent."

Boone's face scrunched into a disbelieving scowl. "Prudent? Dude, there's not enough preplanning and money in the world to pay for that visual so I'm not complaining, but one of the security team could have caught her." He arched a brow. "Of course, I'm still trying to figure out why you were holding her hand in the first place."

Why had he continued to hold her hand? Clay questioned his motivation, ignoring the heat flushing his skin—color he hoped Boone didn't see. He'd held her hand because he wanted to, but he wasn't about to explain that to his cousin. "It just seemed like…" Like what? Like her hand fit in his?

Like he felt protective? Like she needed him? Him. Not Hunt. Not Boone. Not anyone but him. "Like the right thing to do. She was upset. She's a valued member of my staff."

"Oh. So you would have done the same for anyone on staff?"

Clay ignored the other man's smirking grin. "Except you. I'd let you face-plant. What are you getting at?"

"You need to be ready for the media. Georgie needs to be prepared, too. Just sayin'."

"Fine. I'll talk to her so we're on the same page. What time are we scheduled to fly back to DC?"

Boone checked his watch. "You have a meeting there at four." He appeared to be mentally checking the flight time. "We need to leave the hotel within the hour. I'll notify Hunt and Georgie."

Nodding absently, Clay continued to stare out the window. "I'll sit with Georgie on the plane so we can talk."

Unless he was in full campaign mode, he traveled light where personnel was concerned. There would be plenty of room to spread out in the jet for the flight back to DC. He could visit with Georgie with less chance of being overheard. Not that he planned to say anything the others couldn't hear; he just wanted to reassure her. Yes, definitely reassure her. That was what he wanted to do.

Georgie dodged the lead SUV while Clay had his back turned and jumped into the one carrying the luggage and extra security guards. Clay—no, she reminded herself. The senator. He was her boss. She never called him by his first name; that was reserved for her fantasies. Or nightmares, as last night had turned out to be. Call her chicken but she did not want to be in a confined space with him.

On the ride to the airport, she did her best not to think about the puzzled, almost hurt look Clay—the senator—had flashed her direction when he realized she wasn't riding with him. At the hangar, a knot of reporters were waiting on the apron. Georgie grimaced and prepared to do battle with them. This was her job, and she was very good at it, so she needed to just suck it up and get this over with. She was out of the SUV almost before it came to a complete stop. She had her game face on by the time she reached the SUV carrying Clay. One of the security guards jogged in her wake.

"The media will want a statement, Senator. I apologize we didn't have time to discuss preparing one." Yeah, because she was too much of a coward to face him even though Boone said they needed to get their story straight.

"I'll divert the reporters while you go straight to the plane. I'll have something drafted for your approval before we reach Washington." Georgie kept her voice and manner brusque. Professional. Just business as usual. Yeah, right. Nerves thrashed like piranha in a feeding frenzy in her stomach, but she asserted steely control.

The pack was already baying their questions as she plastered her patented I-got-this expression on her face and strolled off to wage a war of wits. She sauntered toward the reporters, held back by a line of uniformed police.

"Georgie! Georgie, hey, Georgie! What's up with you and the senator?"

She arched a brow and stared down her nose at the reporter. Gratified when he squirmed, she rolled her eyes at him. "Seriously, Stu? Since when did you cover the gossip beat?"

"Georgie, what's the senator's stand on that pending eminent domain case in Utah?"

Now this was a slippery slope of a different angle. "As you know, Senator Barron's family have been cattle ranchers for generations. The government coming in to deprive a landowner of his holdings is an issue that should play out in the courts, as this case is doing."

"Georgie, you and the senator sure looked cozy last night at the hotel." A female reporter surged forward, waving her microphone. "Is there something besides business between you two?"

Georgie used her oh-really? face on the reporter. "Trafficking in innuendo now, Jules?"

"The public wants to know, Georgie. Senator Barron is a very eligible bachelor. The two of you work very closely together and I have a source that says you spent the night in his suite."

Georgie forgot to breathe for a moment as she fought to school her expression. According to the Washington press corps, she had one of the best poker faces in the business. She used it now to cover her distress.

"I'm sure all of you are aware of the security breach involving the senator's appearance at the Western States Landowners Association event yesterday. Due to the protection detail's concerns, all members of the senator's immediate traveling party were relocated to the Sonoma Suite, which boasts of amenities for a large group. I'm really disappointed in you, Jules. I thought you were a political reporter. Maybe you and Stu should go to work for *Inquiring Minds*."

She pivoted to leave but one last question caught her attention.

"Yo, Georgie, so this means you aren't dating Senator Barron?"

Glancing over her shoulder, she offered the reporter—a grizzled veteran old enough to be her father—a dazzling smile. "Why, Ed? Do you want to ask me out?"

The reporters all laughed and Georgie made a mental note to send Ed a bottle of good scotch. He'd given her the perfect out and she owed him one. She glanced at the private jet waiting on the tarmac and gulped. Clay stood at the bottom of the steps, arms folded across his chest, feet braced apart. And he looked pissed.

Clay fairly vibrated with anger. Boone cleared his throat and elbowed him. "Smile, Clay. She handled it perfectly. That's why we pay her the big bucks."

"I want the names of those reporters."

"Georgie will have them."

"I don't want her to know I asked for them."

"Dammit, Clay. Take a breath, bud. This is Georgie's job and she does it damn well. Don't muck it up. She handled the situation. Subject closed." Boone angled his head so he could watch Georgie's approach and Clay's expression. "Unless… Clay, please tell me nothing happened between you two."

"Nothing happened between us."

"Well, all-righty, then."

Clay glared when Boone didn't hide his smirk quite fast enough. He ignored his cousin and focused on the woman striding toward them. The bright autumn sun bounced off her glasses. She'd done some twisty thing with her hair again and he didn't want to think too hard about why he preferred it down and loose. She stopped in front of him, her expression perfectly neutral.

"Georgie."

"Senator."

"Sit with me."

Clay noticed the slight pursing of her lips. And was that a hint of panic in her eyes? Interesting. He ushered Georgie forward and followed, his hand resting on the small of her back to steady her. He guided her to the group of seats at the front of the plane. Two pairs of seats faced each other over an inlaid wood table.

Clay guided her into the second set of seats so she'd be sitting with her back to the rest of the plane. Then he nudged her over so that she was trapped between the bulkhead and…him. He slipped her bag off her shoulder and tossed it into one of the facing seats.

"Sit, Georgie. And buckle in. We need to take off."

A few moments later the Rolls Royce engines on the Gulfstream whined to full-throated life and the plane eased onto the apron headed toward the runway. Within minutes they'd lifted off and were at cruising altitude. A vanilla latte appeared in front of her while a cup of black coffee was delivered to Clay. He waited until she took her first swallow before opening the conversation.

"You've been avoiding me. I want to know why."

Georgie grimaced and swallowed hard. He shifted in his seat so he could watch her. A surge of color stained her throat and he wondered about the reason for it. No matter what she did or said, he worried this might not end well. She couldn't stall him. He was determined to find out what was going on in her head, becoming even more curious when she curled her lips between her teeth, pursed them then chewed on them again as she evidently marshaled her thoughts.

She stared into his eyes then glanced away. "I'm a little embarrassed, Senator."

"Embarrassed." Why would the girl—woman—be embarrassed?

"Well, yes. Embarrassed." Though everyone else sat at the rear of the cabin, she dropped her voice. "Last night. In the bathroom."

"Why should you be embarrassed?"

Georgie gave him a scathing look. "Why? Oh, let's recap the situation. I trip and almost fall on my face, only my boss snatches me in mid face-plant and carries me up to his suite. Then I go into full panic mode, while wearing only my underwear, with said boss present to witness said meltdown. I end up in a puddle of tears, and then we make national news. You're right. Why in bloody blue blazes should I be embarrassed?"

Clay was a consummate politician. He knew how to camouflage his emotions. Georgie didn't realize her voice had risen in volume and that everyone on the plane, except maybe the pilots, now knew what had happened in his bathroom. With a supreme effort, he swallowed his laughter.

"Precisely. I see no reason for embarrassment."

"Argh!" She threw up her hands and almost knocked over her latte. He grabbed it and held it out as a peace offering even as she muttered, "Men!" under her breath and gripped the edge of the table.

With gentle pressure, he pried her fingers loose, placed the cup between them and curled her fingers around the porcelain mug. He studied her again as she drank.

She was his communications director. She literally put words in his mouth. His thumb traced lazy circles on the table and a part of him wished it was her skin he touched.

"There's no need to be upset, especially since I…since *we* owe you an apology." She opened her mouth to refute, but he silenced her with a finger touching her lips as he continued. "I personally promise it won't happen again. From now on, Glen will be your shadow whenever we're at a function. He'll protect you." His gaze caught and held hers. "I'm sorry, Georgie. I'm sorry I didn't take care of you."

Georgie couldn't look away from the sincerity in his gaze. She swiveled in her seat so she could face him. His expression stunned her. She'd seen him determined, angry, sad, happy, disgusted…but she'd never seen him like this. Her stomach lurched as her pulse sped up. Georgie couldn't name the emotion in his eyes with their thick, dark lashes the color of his ebony hair. In her imagination, where her fantasies lived, she described his hair in romance-novel terms—as glossy as a raven's wing. And his eyes—burnt umber, even if she didn't really know what burnt umber looked like. It sounded sexy and that term definitely fit Clay. Or cognac. Yes, that was the color. She knew what cognac looked like in a leaded glass tumbler and his eyes looked like that—smoky, swirling brown with glinting lights. Lost in his gaze, she simply took him in, letting him fill her up. The force of him edged into the empty places she'd ignored her whole life, the places where her hopes and dreams lived.

I'm in so much trouble now. Having a crush on the man was one thing, but she feared that after this trip, she'd fallen way over her head in love with her boss. She cleared her throat, dragging her gaze from his to break their connection. She managed to say one word.

"Okay."

Another emotion flickered across his expression, lightening his mood. "Okay. Good. Then we're all settled. How about some breakfast?"

Breakfast. Yes, breakfast would work to put some distance between them and let her get her fantasies back under control. "Okay."

He patted her arm. "For a woman whose job is words, you seem to have very few of them at the moment."

They were somewhere over Tennessee when Georgie fell asleep. She dreamed of Clay, of him slipping his arm over her shoulders to pull her against his side.

"Georgie?" He whispered her name.

"What?" She whispered back.

"I think I'm going to kiss you now."

She sighed, wanting to feel his lips on hers. "You think?"

"I know I want to."

"Okay."

"Okay?"

"Um...yeah. Okay." Inside the dream she wanted to bang

her head on the table. What was up with her managing to only say *okay*?

She focused on his mouth. Full lips. Firm. Hints of smile lines at the corners.

He plucked her glasses from the end of her nose and set them aside on the table. The corner of his mouth quirked as he looked at her.

"What will you taste like?" dream Clay asked. "Dessert sweet and rich? Or twenty-year-old scotch, a smoky burn in my mouth? I can't wait to find out."

He lowered his head and his lips brushed across hers. She licked her bottom lip, her tongue darting out to sample the taste of him. He moved in again, no hesitation this time. His lips fastened onto hers, sucking in her bottom lip as his teeth nipped. One hand secured the back of her head, angling it to the perfect position for his tender attack.

Normally bold in her fantasies about Clay, she now felt shy and her actions mirrored her emotions. Her hands, hesitant and timid, latched onto his leather jacket—he always wore leather in her dreams—and clung there as though her life depended on it. Emotions rushed through her and a little voice said she should run. Ignoring it, Georgie pressed into their kiss, her tongue now bold enough to dance with his—until he pulled away.

"Georgie, wake up. We're getting ready to land." Breathing hard, she opened her eyes to discover that Clay was watching her, amusement twitching his lips into a sexy grin.

"Oh, pistachios on pita. Please tell me I wasn't talking in my sleep."

Four

Clay smoothed his features into a neutral expression. He *had* heard his name on her lips several times, and the little smooching noises and puckering of her lips was both cute and...arousing. While he'd surely like to know the details, there would be a time and place to discover what Georgie dreamed about—and specifically his role in those dreams—but this wasn't it.

"Do you make a habit of talking in your sleep?" He snapped his mouth shut, shocked he'd pursued the subject.

Georgie pushed her glasses up her nose and stared at him. Her forehead crinkled and her lips pursed as she gave the question serious thought. "I...don't know, seeing as I'm usually asleep. Would you like me to set up a recorder to find out?"

She looked so serious, Clay hesitated a few seconds before laughing. He opened his mouth to say the first thing that popped into his head, but stopped as innate political instincts kicked in. Offering to watch her sleep at night was not a smart move. He relayed a stern warning to all interested body parts. Georgie was an employee and off-limits. Period.

"Would you?" He wanted to head-slap himself. And shut up. Yes, keeping his mouth shut would be a good thing right about now.

"Ah, Clay?"

Boone. Thank goodness. His cousin could always be counted on to pull his butt out of the fire. Clay turned away from Georgie and focused on his chief of staff. "What's up?"

Boone had to clear his throat before speaking and he wouldn't quite meet Clay's gaze. The words that came out were strained as he tried to stifle his laughter. "Transport is waiting at the airport. We'll head straight to the office. And you have an email from your sister-in-law."

"Cassidy?"

"Only sister-in-law I'm aware of."

"What about?"

"Thanksgiving."

"Thanksgiving?"

"Yes. As in, are we coming home for the holidays? A question also being asked repeatedly by my mother."

"I don't have time."

Boone glanced toward Georgie. "Take Georgie home with you. Make it a long working weekend. And give her time to slide home to see her dad."

"My dad?" Georgie sounded surprised. "Thanksgiving? He and his buddies go hunting in Montana every year."

Studying her for a long moment, Clay considered his next comment. "Sounds like your Thanksgivings are a lot like mine. Boone, email Cassie and tell her I'll be in touch for the details."

After Boone returned to his seat and buckled up, Clay noticed Georgie's hands were a little white-knuckled as she gripped the table. "Problem?"

"I don't like landings. Takeoffs? Not thrilled but I'm fine. Landings?" She blinked at him a few times and her bangs brushed the tops of her glasses as she wrinkled her forehead. "Yeah, not so much."

Prying one hand free, he laced his fingers through hers. "Good to know I'm not the only one." He squeezed gently. "Hold my hand to make me feel better? Boone gets all weird when I ask him to do it."

An odd little noise that was a cross between a giggle and snort burst from her and she tucked her teeth between her pressed lips to hold back the full laugh. "I can imagine."

Her green eyes flashed in the sunlight streaming through

the plane window as the pilot banked to line up on the runway. “Don’t tell my constituents.”

She gestured with her free hand, miming zipping her lips, pressing them closed. “Mmm nnnllps er hhed.”

“Your lips are sealed?”

Georgie nodded vigorously. “We wouldn’t want the voters to know their favorite senator is a ’fraidy cat.”

“Good to know I can trust you.” It struck him then. He *could* trust Georgie. She’d become an integral part of his inner cadre but he’d never considered the trust he bestowed on her as she moved into her current position. He reflected on what he knew of her. While usually on the quiet side, she didn’t back down easily when she believed herself to be right. And she had a wicked sense of humor, most often directed at Boone.

A flash of jealousy zinged through him. Was there something between Boone and Georgie? Boone called her *sugar*. All the time. Damn it. But if there was something going on, why should Clay care?

The plane touched down and the engines whined as the pilot applied brakes, diverting him from his thoughts.

Leaving the ground crew to deal with luggage, Clay, Boone and Georgie headed toward his senate offices, driven by Glen with Hunter riding shotgun. The SUV forged through the typically heavy Washington traffic, bullying its way from Dulles to the Russell Senate Office Building in a drive that took almost forty-five minutes. Turning left onto Delaware, the vehicle rolled to a smooth stop just past the main entrance on the southwest corner of the building.

Hunt was out of the front seat and opening doors even as his eyes roved the surroundings in a threat assessment. As Boone stepped out first, his brother tilted his head. “Shark at three o’clock.”

Boone snorted as he helped Georgie and then Clay out. “Parker Grace is headed this way.”

"Senator! Senator Barron!"

Georgie schooled her features to keep her thoughts from leaking into her expression. A reporter for a local television station, Parker Grace scurried toward them, her four-inch heels clattering against the concrete sidewalk. With her perfectly coiffed platinum hair and inch-long eyelashes fluttering over blue eyes, the woman was always the epitome of feminine perfection. And Georgie hated her for it.

Parker's gaze flicked over her and then focused on Clay. "Senator, do you care to make a comment about your affair with a staff member?"

Sugar would have melted on the woman's tongue, but the vinegar beneath her words soured Georgie's stomach. She stepped up beside Clay, prepared to do her job, but Boone cut her off.

"Really, Parker? You get demoted to the gossip beat or something?"

The woman flushed but kept her microphone waving toward Clay. "Those pictures from Scottsdale are fairly explicit, Senator, and word has leaked out that Ms..." The reporter's gaze once again washed over Georgie and dismissed her. "Your...assistant was seen leaving your suite after spending the night there. Care to comment?"

Once again, Boone cut Georgie off and she fumed at being usurped. "Parker, Parker, Parker. Did your sources also say that I was staying in the same suite, in my capacity as the senator's chief of staff, along with his security chief, other security personnel and Ms. Dreyfus, the senator's communications director?"

Georgie couldn't remain silent any longer. "Seriously, Grace? You want to go there?"

"Most people would, Dreyfus. How wonderfully *Fifty Shades*. The mousy press secretary and the handsome, powerful senator."

Georgie laughed. "Oh, apple pie, my eye. What have

you been smoking?" Georgie gripped the woman's arm and tugged her away from the others, though the cameraman followed. Lowering her voice, she fluttered her lashes in perfect imitation of Parker. "Ooh, Senator, I'd love to get my gold-digging claws into your trust fund."

The guy with the camera huffed out a snort and rolled his eyes as Georgie stepped even closer to the reporter, her palm covering the microphone. "You want to get up and personal with me, Grace, bring it. But this vendetta you have because you threw yourself at the senator and he had the good taste to ignore you needs to stop. Don't make me go to your producers."

Arching a brow, Georgie waited. She had information Parker didn't—mainly that Barron Entertainment owned the majority shares in the station the reporter worked for. And she was fairly positive that a word to Boone would result in a phone call to Chase Barron, Barron Entertainment CEO.

"Don't threaten me, Georgeanne Dreyfus," the other woman hissed. When Georgie just continued to stare, Parker blanched. "You wouldn't dare."

"Let's get everything out in the open, Parker. When it comes to the senator, there's very little I wouldn't dare. I'm telling you unequivocally there is not, nor has there ever been anything of a romantic nature between Senator Barron and me. If you want to go fishing in that pond, be careful what bait you use. You never know what you might catch on the end of your line. Some things out there in the water bite. Hard."

Parker assessed her with a questioning eye but Georgie didn't flinch. "When did you get so tough, little girl?"

"Honey, I'm an Oklahoma cowgirl. We're born tough. And don't you forget it." Georgie offered the cameraman a sympathetic look as Parker stormed away, her ridiculous heels tap-tap-tapping on the pavement. “Yeah, good luck with that.”

He snorted again and with a resigned slump of his shoulders, followed the retreating talent.

“I *am* still capable of speaking for myself, Georgie.”

Startled by the voice in her ear, she whirled and almost tipped over when she bumped into Clay—who was standing inordinately close. Heat crept up her cheeks and she settled her glasses more firmly on her nose. “The last time I checked, talking to reporters is still in my job description.”

“So…Parker had a thing for me, huh?”

Her mouth dropped open and she closed it, only to gape again as Boone chuckled and nudged Clay’s shoulder with his. “I *told* you so.” He held out his hand. “Pay up, cuz.”

Georgie snapped her mouth shut again. “Wait…you made a *bet*? On what?”

While Boone tried to look innocent, she didn’t fall for it. “Please don’t tell me you were betting on me confronting her.”

A wickedly sinful grin spread across Clay’s face. “Okay. We won’t tell you.” He snagged her arm and headed toward the building’s entrance. “But I would appreciate knowing the next time a sexy woman finds me desirable. Men need to know these things.”

Sputtering, Georgie allowed Clay to tow her along beside him. Jealousy flared hot as a sparkler on the 4th of July and she stuffed it deep. As they entered the Russell’s rotunda, Clay leaned down to whisper in her ear.

“And for your information, I find nothing mousy about you.”

Three weeks later Clay sprawled in the desk chair in the study at the Barron family compound in Oklahoma City, feet propped on the scarred desktop. Despite his busy schedule, he’d caved to his sister-in-law’s demand for a family Thanksgiving gathering. He'd insisted it was a working break and brought Georgie with him. They were currently dealing with his upcoming schedule. Georgie, all business, stood at the whiteboard ticking off a list when his nephew plowed into the room. "Uncle Clay! Aunt Cassie says time to eat. You gots to come now, 'kay?" The boy was all but bouncing out of his cowboy boots and Clay wasn't quite sure how to respond. Cord, his next younger brother, had almost died earlier in the fall. During his recovery, he'd reconnected—sort of—with his ex-girlfriend, only to discover he had a son. CJ looked like a Barron and Clay remembered when Cord and Chance had been filled with the same energy.

He'd been their caretaker during their mother's final illness and death from cancer. Their father hadn't wanted to deal with the domestic situation so he didn't. Cyrus Barron had done what he did best: abandoned his parental responsibilities. And after the accidental death of his first stepmother, Clay had also taken on the twins, Chase and Cash, when Cyrus pulled his disappearing act.

Dropping his feet to the floor, Clay pushed out of the chair and joined CJ at the door. "You heard the little man, Georgie. Aunt Cassie says it's time to eat." He ruffled the boy's hair. "Has your dad explained about the wishbone?"

CJ's eyes widened and he nodded like a bobblehead dog on the dash of a car driving down a rough road. "Yup. Uncle Cash 'n' me get to break it an' I get something cool when I win. C'mon! There's pie and hot rolls and sweet taters."

Holding the door, Clay gestured for Georgie to precede him, a part of him oddly gratified she'd agreed to come home with him for the weekend. Granted, they'd mostly been closeted in this small study since their arrival the previous day so he hadn't had much interaction with anyone besides her, but wasn't that the point? She was a buffer between him and his brothers, in much the same way that she stood between him and the press.

The meal went as family gatherings usually did in the Barron household, at least when Cyrus was absent—lots of teasing, gooey glances between Chance and his not-so-new bride as Miz Beth and Big John presided over the festivities like the surrogate parents they'd been since coming into the brothers' lives. When the time came for the wishbone pull, Cash—as the youngest brother—made a half-hearted attempt at the tradition with CJ. When the boy won, Cash pushed away from the table and strode out, angry over something.

Clay considered following his baby brother but CJ's sly wish about getting his mom and dad back together kept him in his seat as Cord stammered his way through an explanation of why that wouldn't happen. With the cleanup underway and football-watching to follow, Clay took the opportunity to slip back into the study.

Almost two hours later his father strode in. Clay glanced up at the intrusion, surprised since Chance had assured everyone that Cyrus was in Las Vegas for the duration. He sat up straighter, recognizing the set of the man's shoulders and the expression on his face.

"We need to talk." The old man glowered, anticipating he'd vacate the chair behind the desk. Clay didn't indulge him.

Irritated now more than when he'd walked in, his old man lowered himself into a less comfortable chair and didn't wait to fire the opening volley. "Get your brothers. We have family business."

Clay didn't like the derisive tone in his father's voice. "What sort of *family* business?"

"Cord and my grandson and that woman who wants to ruin them both. Now get the hell out of my chair. We'll talk more after I deal with your thickheaded brother."

Doing as he was told but dragging his feet, he went in search of his brothers. He found Cash first and received a curt nod and sneer for his trouble. "I'll round up everyone and then text Cord to meet us in the conference room," Cash informed him.

Cash's reaction and obvious previous knowledge of the situation left a bitter taste in Clay's mouth. His youngest brother had once been the most easygoing of them all—rivaling even Cord for being laid-back. He wondered what had happened to turn Cash into the man he currently was.

With reluctance, Clay headed to the conference room and sank into the chair at one end of the table. During the "family intervention" his father demanded Cord sue for full custody of CJ, and made other more personal demands about CJ's mother, Jolie. It left Clay slightly angered—at his father, at his baby brother, but proud of Cord and Chance for standing up to the old man. He should probably do the same, though a heavy sense of dread hung over him as he followed his father back into the study.

"What are your plans?"

"My plans for what?"

"The election."

"As you well know, I'm forming an exploratory committee."

"You need to declare early. Scare off the competition."

"This may not be the right cycle to run."

"Bull. You will campaign, get the party's nomination, and we'll make a successful run at the presidency."

"We," Clay said in a clipped tone, letting the pronoun hang in the emotionally charged atmosphere.

"I can't trust you not to mess it up. I'll be there every step of the way. I have some things to deal with here but I'll be in Washington next week. We'll get things started."

Despite the urge, and a certain need to do so, Clay didn't argue. A smart man picked his battles with the old man. This wasn't the time or the place.

Five

Even now, late on a snowy December day when his colleagues were preparing to flee Washington for their home districts, Clay glared at the files highlighted in the pool of stark white LED light shining on his desk. He pretended he was too busy to make it home for the holidays but in reality, he didn't want to deal with the family drama happening back in Oklahoma. The intervention at Thanksgiving involving Cord, the mother of his child and the boy himself soured Clay's stomach. As much as he'd enjoyed meeting his nephew and reconnecting with his brothers, overall, succumbing to his new sister-in-law's plea to appear for the family gathering had been an unmitigated disaster. And he still had his old man all up in his political business.

A peal of laughter floated through his half-opened office door. Georgie. She'd been the one high point in the Thanksgiving travesty. He'd all but begged her to accompany him, his excuse that she was the best speechwriter on the Hill and he had precampaign stops to make on the way back to Washington. In truth, he'd needed her there to insulate him from the dysfunction surrounding his family. Her presence and clear head kept him centered.

A male voice rumbled in the background and Georgie laughed again. A streak of jealousy twisted through him before he clamped down on his emotions. Georgie was an employee. He didn't fish in the office pond. Ever. Unlike many of his associates. He closed the file he'd been studying—the oil and gas production bill wasn't going anywhere anytime soon—and wondered who was in the reception area with her. He kept a skeleton staff during December. While Congress didn't officially break for Christmas recess until

December twenty-first, the Hill effectively ground to a stop in anticipation of the holiday weeks before.

A few moments later Boone rapped on the door and stuck his head in. "Dude, enough. We need steaks. And beer."

The Tate brothers belonged to Clay's aunt Katherine, his father's sister. While all of them carried the trademark Barron dark hair, they'd inherited their father's blue eyes, and Boone's twinkled with good humor. He stepped fully into the office and glanced over his shoulder. "I bet I can convince Georgie to come with us, since we three are the only ones still here." He waggled his brows and Clay couldn't help but chuckle at his cousin's antics.

When his stomach grumbled in agreement, Clay surrendered. As long as Boone was there to chaperone, he could keep his mind on business and not on the woman whose presence had inexplicably begun to make his breath catch and his thoughts wander to places they had no business visiting. "Are you buyin'?"

A snort of laughter was quickly followed by a shake of Boone's head. "Hell no, cuz. You're the one who makes the big bucks. We have reservations at Max's Steakhouse and we're going to miss them. Now, get your butt in gear."

The woman under discussion breezed into the room, a quiet smile on her face. She pushed the heavy black frames of her glasses up on her nose. "Did you convince him he needs beef?"

Georgie's voice did funny things to Clay—most of them centered below the belt buckle. She interacted with the press often and he'd overheard one male journalist comment that Georgie had the voice of a phone sex operator, but the rest of her didn't follow through. He'd studied Georgie following that crack and came to his own conclusion. Who knew girls in glasses looked so sexy? Thank goodness no one saw her the same way he did. He'd hate to start a fistfight.

Which was so outside the realm of his normal behavior he now second-guessed every word, thought and action where Georgie was concerned.

She'd been a fixture in his office almost since the beginning, recruited by Boone first as a campaign assistant and then as a deputy press secretary after her graduation from the University of Oklahoma's journalism school. Since that time, she'd worked her way through the ranks. After her comments regarding her own Thanksgiving and family, Clay had done a little covert checking. Her mother had been a Tulsa socialite who met and married Georgie's father in college. They'd divorced when Georgie was thirteen, after living apart most of her life. Marlena Dreyfus had hated life on the ranch. After the divorce she had moved to Dallas, and effectively ignored her daughter. George Dreyfus had raised his daughter to be a cowgirl until Georgie departed for college and then joined Clay's staff.

Putting Hunt on the trail, he learned Georgie had had one semiserious boyfriend in college, and seldom dated anyone more than a few times since coming to Washington. The idea she didn't have many men in her past pleased Clay, and he was man enough to admit that was his ego talking because he had a whole string of women peppering his past. Clay was also honest enough to admit his sudden interest was closer to stalking than infatuation. But he didn't care. Georgie was an important and trusted member of his staff. He should know these things. And finding out about her had nothing to do with the vivid dreams in which she starred, leaving him hard and wanting upon awaking. No, those dreams had nothing at all to do with his current curiosity.

"Who's driving?" Boone was shrugging into his sheepskin coat as he glared out the window into the Russell Building's inner courtyard. Snow fell thick and fast.

"Not you," Georgie teased. "I called Hunt earlier. He's

sending an SUV for us. Four-wheel drive. And he promised a driver who knows how to navigate in this stuff."

"Well, that certainly makes me feel safer." Clay jingled the keys in his coat pocket. He'd much rather drive—not that he was a control freak. Much. Georgie was smart to get a ride for them. Washingtonians and winter driving didn't mix when it came to maneuvering the streets of DC. He grabbed his topcoat from the old-fashioned coat rack in the corner while Georgie ducked out to her office to grab her own coat.

They nodded to the guard as they left the building and strode straight to the black Suburban idling next to the curb. Georgie ended up sandwiched between him and Boone in the backseat. Clay's thigh pressed against hers and he heard her breath hitch. Glancing at her, he caught the flushing of her creamy skin, obvious even in the darkness of the winter night. Interesting.

Hunt twisted around in the front to look at them. "Jeez. Did I forget my deodorant or something? Nobody fighting over who gets to ride shotgun?"

"What are you doing here?" Clay was surprised to see his chief of security in the driver's seat.

"Georgie said you were buying. At Max's. That means good beef. Hell yeah, I'm driving."

Boone laughed and jumped out, ducking into the front passenger seat a moment later. "I'll sit up here, bro, since you're such a big baby about riding all by your lonesome."

The brothers argued good-naturedly during the drive to the restaurant. Clay breathed shallowly because Georgie had barely moved into the seat vacated by Boone. She was close enough their shoulders brushed each time Hunt turned a corner. And that was so not good. Boundaries. Clay needed them. Not to mention he had plans of the romantic variety over the holiday break. A Broadway star was anticipating his presence as her escort at a variety of glittering parties in New York and Boston. Parties where the rich and powerful would be. Parties where he would make contacts to further his political aspirations and allow him to test the waters surrounding his run for the party's presidential nomination.

When they were seated in a round booth inside Max's a few minutes later, the brotherly banter continued. Clay envied his cousins. Aunt Katherine could be a domineering matriarch but she also baked cookies, was a staunch supporter of her children and loved them fiercely. He remembered his own mother as being weak and subservient to the old man. She'd loved him and his brothers in her own way, and they'd loved her. When Cyrus had married his stepmother Helen, she'd done her best to mother him, Cord and Chance, but she'd become pregnant fairly soon after the wedding and the twins kept her crazy busy. Until that fateful rainy day when a drunk driver and a blind curve had changed everything.

Georgie nudged him with her shoulder. "Penny for your thoughts?"

He scowled at her for a moment. "They aren't worth that much." Which was true. Introspection never did him any good. He tuned back in to the conversation. Boone and Hunt were going at it again, claiming each was their mother's favorite.

"My Christmas present will be the biggest." Folding his arms across his chest, Hunt smirked at Boone.

"Nuh-uh. Mine will be. Mom loves me best because I'm cutest."

Hunt snickered. "You know that's not true! That claim belongs to Deacon. Mom has always thought he was the cutest."

"That's because he's a *star*." Boone rolled his eyes as he made air quotes around the last word. "She just wants to go to the Country Music Association Awards with him."

Clay snorted, getting into the conversation. "Deke taking Aunt Katherine to the CMAs? Riiight. Not gonna happen. That boy has girls draped around him like his momma's mink stole."

Boone reached across Georgie and punched Clay's shoulder with a loose fist. "Just like someone else I know. When are you headed up to New York to see Giselle?"

After checking the calendar on his phone, Clay shrugged. "We're scheduled for a charity reception at the Plaza on the eighteenth. I'll probably fly up that morning."

The conversation paused as their waiter appeared and delivered their plates. The men all dug into their steaks and baked potatoes with gusto. Georgie was a bit daintier as she cut and chewed. The excellent medium-rare Angus beef almost melting in her mouth wasn't the only thing she chewed over.

Clay was still seeing Giselle Richards, the Tony award–winning actress from Oklahoma. That discovery shouldn't have surprised her. Except Clay seldom dated anyone for longer than a few months. Giselle had been on his horizon for almost nine. Georgie kept her eyes on her plate and worked to keep all expression off her face. Clay dated. This was a fact of life. She had absolutely no claim on him outside the office. Period. Her life was simpler that way. And her heart infinitely safer.

The men continued talking as the food disappeared from their plates.

Boone nudged her foot under the table. "Yo, Georgie, you're way too quiet."

She frowned and huffed. "Too quiet? With you three, who can get a word in edgewise?"

All three men chuckled and Hunt jostled Boone. "Ha. She's got your number, little bro."

"My number?" Boone pointed to his chest. "One." He pointed at Hunt then Clay. "Two. Three. She said, and I quote, 'With you *three*.' I think she knows us all extremely well."

Georgie glanced at her wristwatch. "Because I do, I'm going to skedaddle before this conversation deteriorates any further."

She stared at Boone as a hint to slide out of the booth so she could exit. He didn't move. She cleared her throat and Boone pointedly ignored her. Then his leg brushed across her shins. Clay jerked and stared at her. Her eyes wide, she turned her head to narrow them at Boone. "You will pay for that. Now move." She shoved at his shoulder.

Hunt slid out. "I'll take my little brother's hint. You aren't walking to the Metro. We'll drive you home."

"Good idea, bro."

A few minutes later, the tab paid, coats claimed and the valet dispatched, the four of them waited just inside the door. When the SUV pulled up, they headed out. Feeling ornery, Georgie headed around the front of the vehicle. "Shotgun!"

She caught all three men flat-footed and was ensconced in the front seat before they reacted. Hunt laughed as he climbed in behind the wheel, flashing smug looks at the other men. Georgie felt inordinately proud of herself even as she faced the thought of a confrontation with Boone. He'd been nudging Clay and her together. A lot. He needed to stop his romantic machinations immediately because… well…because!

When Hunt pulled up in front of her apartment building, Clay was out of the backseat and at her door before she could get it open. She was about to argue but he had her arm, tugging her onto the sidewalk.

"I'll walk you inside."

Six

Clay cupped Georgie's elbow with one hand while his other automatically went to the small of her back. The sidewalk was slippery. That was his excuse. She turned at the door to say good-night and he suddenly realized he didn't want her to go.

Jumping in before she could dismiss him, he said, "I'll walk you up to your apartment."

"Senator—"

"Clay."

Her lips parted slightly and he wondered if that was an invitation. Nope, he shouldn't go there. Just…

"Really, Senator, I'm fine. This is a secure building and you really don't want to hike up three flights."

And she put him right back in his place. Georgie was right, of course. He was taking off in a few days to spend the holidays with Giselle. His ironclad policy was no office shenanigans. This sudden interest in the woman who'd been under his nose for years was just…an infatuation. Or something. He curled his fingers into his palms to keep from cupping her face.

"Then I'll say good night, Georgie. See you in the office tomorrow morning."

Some emotion he couldn't quite define flickered across her expression, gone before he could capture it. He stepped back so he wouldn't do something stupid. Like kiss her while standing there on the stoop with Boone and Hunt watching from the SUV.

The lock snicked and she pushed the door open. "Good night…Senator." Georgie slipped through the opening before he could change his mind and she shut the door behind her, locking him out. He stood in the cold, his breath fogging the glass until she turned into the stairwell and disappeared from his sight. He stepped out on the sidewalk, head craned back, waiting. A few minutes later lights illuminated a set of windows on the third floor and Georgie's shadow passed across them.

The back window of the SUV slithered down and Boone leaned out. "Yo, Clay, get in the car. It's freezing."

With a reluctance he didn't quite understand, Clay settled into the front passenger seat. Silence reigned for about thirty seconds and then his cousins erupted in laughter.

"Idiots," he muttered under his breath.

"Who, us?" Boone reached between the seats to slug his shoulder. "Clay, you need to ask that girl out."

"No."

"Why not?"

"Isn't it obvious? She works for me, Boone."

"No, technically she works for me."

"And you work for me. Just...forget it. Bad idea. You're the one who pointed this out in Arizona. Besides, she doesn't—" He bit off the rest of the sentence.

"She doesn't what? Like you? Jeez, Clay. You are so freaking dense sometimes. That girl has crushed on you from the moment she walked in the door. And I only asked if you knew what you were doing in Scottsdale."

Hunt glanced over and rolled his eyes. "Huh. Are we like in junior high now?"

"Shut up, Hunt. And you, too, Boone." Clay held up his hand, cutting off their jibes. "In fact, I think I'll fly up to New York tomorrow. Hunt, make sure the plane is available and Boone, if you'll make arrangements at the Waldorf, I'd appreciate it."

Hunt looked as if he was going to say something else, but closed his mouth and grimaced before saying, "I'll instruct Cash to have a security team meet you."

"Good. I'll leave straight from home in the morning. You two can take care of the office until the winter recess."

The SUV rolled to a stop in front of Clay's Georgetown townhouse. The gray-painted brick building was almost obscured by the snow drifting down. The red brick sidewalk was completely covered. DC would be shut down by morning.

"Crap. Boone, email the staff and tell them to stay home tomorrow. There's no way the streets will be plowed. And that means I'll delay the trip to New York by a day."

"You realize you're running away, right?"

Hunt chimed in with chicken noises.

"Just do what I ordered." Clay climbed out and stomped through the snow to the wrought-iron gate protecting his small yard and entrance door. The black vehicle idled at the curb while he fought the accumulated snow to get the gate open and closed. The motion detector installed with his security system lit up the interior as he approached the door, keyed in the code and entered.

He decided to ignore the juvenile antics of his cousins. This was a matter of discretion being the better part of valor. Yes, he was tempted by Georgie but she was an employee. She was also the best speechwriter on the Hill and he was *not* going to jeopardize that relationship to pursue one of a more intimate nature.

Georgie opened her door, shoved a large, steaming mug into the hands of the woman standing there and ushered her inside. The trip up from the second floor hadn't taken her best friend long.

"Why are adult snow days not near as much fun as when we were kids and got to stay home from school?" Jen groused as she shuffled in on fuzzy house shoe–clad feet. She let loose with a huge yawn before sipping the hot chocolate in her mug. "Ooh. You put cinnamon in it."

"Of course I did. Do you want breakfast?"

"What do you have?"

Wandering into her small kitchen, Georgie checked the fridge and the cabinets. "Uhm…two boiled eggs. Instant oatmeal. And coffee."

"Put marshmallows in my next hot chocolate and we'll call it brunch." Jen settled on Georgie's couch, propped her feet on the coffee table and yawned again. "So talk to me."

Georgie topped off her coffee and curled up on the opposite end of the overstuffed couch, doing her best to seem as though she was okay. "About what?"

"Why you look so bummed out. Duh."

"I'm not bummed."

"Oh? Really? Coulda fooled me. What's up with the Oklahoma Stud?"

Blushing furiously, Georgie kicked at Jen's thigh. "Don't call him that."

"Then tell me what's going on between you two."

"Nothing." She barely avoided a sigh. "The office went to dinner last night and he walked me to the door."

"Did he kiss you?"

"Jen! Stop it! No. He did not. We don't have a…a relationship like that."

"And whose fault is that?"

Georgie stuck her fingers in her ears and sang, "La-la-la-la-la. Not listening to you."

"You know you want him, girl."

"He's my boss. And…" She pushed her glasses back to the bridge of her nose. "He's spending Christmas in New York. With Giselle Richards. And last night he told me he'd see me tomorrow…meaning today. Except he decided to leave early for New York and was going straight to the airport except…snow day."

Jen's face smoothed out and sympathy filled her gaze. "Well…that sucks."

"Yeah."

"Are they like…a thing?"

"He's been seeing her since…Valentine's Day."

"Wait. Their first date was Valentine's Day? Who does that?"

"It wasn't a date. Exactly. She was his escort for some deal at the Western Heritage Center in Oklahoma City. They went to the same high school or something."

"*Pffft*. She's got nothin' on you, Georgie."

"Says my best friend who is loyal to a fault. But have you seen her? She's a former Miss America and she won the Tony two years ago and she's gorgeous and…and…" Georgie couldn't swallow her sigh this time. "You know he's putting together an exploratory committee, right?" At Jen's nod, she continued. "Giselle is the type of woman he needs on his arm when he runs for president. She knows what to say to people. Looks amazing. Doesn't trip and fall over her own feet. Or wear glasses."

"I call BS."

"Why? She's beautiful and talented and…everything I'm not."

"And she's a total airhead. Have you ever heard her interviewed? I mean, seriously. I don't know what Senator Barron sees in her."

Georgie stared at Jen, all but gaping. "You are so not a guy. She walks by and their tongues hang out."

"Well, you're smart and funny and…and sweet and… and…"

"And nothing. I invited you over to cheer me up."

"It's too early in the morning. And there's no ice cream."

"I know. I'm a lousy hostess, which just proves my point." Georgie curled her upper lip and rolled her eyes, which made Jen laugh, as she'd intended. "At least Christmas is almost here. I'll go home. Stuff myself on Dad's turkey and dressing and drown my sorrows in giblet gravy."

"That's the spirit!"

* * *

Clay kicked back in the deep leather chair, his feet propped up on the matching ottoman. He negligently held a lead crystal glass with two fingers of scotch in one hand. Boone had decided to stay at the ranch with him while everyone else headed to downtown Oklahoma City to ring in the New Year.

"We didn't expect you for the holidays, cuz."

"Yeah. Staying in New York wasn't really an option."

"You give Giselle the boot?"

"Nope."

"She kicked you out?" Boone perked up and leaned forward. "This'll be good."

"Yeah, well." Clay lifted one shoulder in a forcibly nonchalant shrug before sipping the aged whiskey in his glass. "Not smart to forget a woman's name in the middle of things."

"You forgot Giselle's name? Oh, dude. You *are* a dog. That's what pet names are for, right?"

"Worse than that, Boone."

The other man stared at him, eyes crinkling and his mouth curling into a smirk as he figured it out. "Oh, hell, ol' son. Please don't tell me you called her by another woman's name..."

Clay did his best to maintain a poker face, but knew he'd failed the moment Boone burst out laughing. "It's not funny."

"Is, too."

"Is not."

Boone controlled his laughter but still smirked. "Whose name?" Blinking several times, the full impact hit him. "Oh, crap. Georgie."

Clay figured he looked as miserable as he felt. "How screwed up am I, Boone?"

"I don't think you're screwed up at all, man. Georgie is

a gem. Granted, she's not a supermodel, but she's got that whole sexy librarian thing, plus no one is smarter and her zingers are worth the price of admission. I mean, seriously. Why are you just now seeing what the rest of us saw from the git-go?"

"I'm a slow learner. However, I *am* seeing it now so what the hell do I do about it?"

"Simple. Ask her out."

"I can't."

"Why not? I mean, seriously, cuz, what's the problem?"

"I'd have to fire her. Which sucks because she's the best communications director on the Hill. And there's no guarantee we'd last longer than a fling. If she'd even go for it. Doesn't sound like a win-win for anybody."

"I don't follow, Clay. Why would you have to fire her? And I'm not even going into fling territory."

Draining his drink, Clay laid his head against the back of the chair and closed his eyes. "The old man, Boone. Every bit of fluff he brought into the house came from his office. The side pieces, the step-monsters he dragged in—each one younger than the previous. Well, except for Helen. She wanted to be a mom. The rest? Gold diggers, every last one."

He rubbed his fingers over his forehead, but the headache brewing behind his eyes didn't go away. "I swore I would never be him."

"So you date supermodels and actresses and pretty women who are dumber than stumps because you don't want to follow in his footsteps? I have four names for you, starting with Tammy."

Clay groaned. "Lord, that cost us a pretty penny to get rid of her, and she took the foreman with her. Thank goodness Chance made sure she signed the prenup. Besides, I wasn't referring to the quality of the women I date but where I meet them. I refuse to have an office romance."

"Then fire Georgie."

Resisting the urge to throw the now-empty glass at his cousin, Clay heaved out of the chair and went to the bar to pour another, stiffer drink. "I don't want to lose her, Boone." He tossed back the drink, barely resisting the urge to slam the glass down on the marble bar top. "I don't know what to do."

"I do. Just trust me on this."

Seven

Georgie blinked rapidly, the seldom-worn contacts irritating her eyes. She longed to take them out and stick her glasses back on. Resisting, she used drops while managing not to smear her makeup. She had to be crazy. When Boone had called with a last-minute request, she thought, *why not?* That was before she'd dressed up. Now she stood there in panic mode.

Returning to the senate offices after the holiday break had been…interesting. Boone and Hunt intimated that Clay had cut his New York trip short and spent the holidays at the family ranch north of Oklahoma City. She was curious enough to wonder if Clay had broken up with Giselle and she tried very hard to quell any internal squee moments that thought created. He was so far out of Georgie's league that…

The notes of "Girls Just Want to Have Fun" drifted in from her bedroom. She staggered on her high heels, found the impossibly small and expensive evening bag Jen had loaned her and snagged her cell phone.

"Do not have time, Jen. Go away."

"Breathe, Georgie. Things will be fine." Her best friend unleashed a sultry chuckle. "In fact, I bet he takes you back to his place for a nightcap."

"Oh, sure. Right. The man is handsome enough to be a movie star, he's a gazillionaire and he always dates the most beautiful socialites and supermodels in the world. I, on the other hand, am me. I am so totally average that the political pollsters have my type on speed dial. Men like Senator Barron do not make passes at girls who wear glasses and work in their office. One, it is a huge breach of ethics and two…have you looked at me, Jen? Yes, you're my best friend in the whole world and you love me, but let's be real. I won't ever win a beauty contest."

The buzzer sounded, alerting her that someone was at the outer door to her building, and she cut off Jen's reply. "Gotta go."

Time was up. Smoothing the formal gown, she grabbed a warm wrap and the beaded bag.

Using the same care as a tightrope walker, she managed both the apartment building's stairs and entryway without tripping on the high heels she normally avoided wearing. Her feet would kill her before the night was over but such was the price of fashion.

Boone waited beside the limo and his eyes lit up when she emerged from the door. "Dang, sugar. You clean up real nice."

His exaggerated accent made her laugh and relax. Boone always managed to walk the fine line between boss and friend. He kept up a running commentary on the way to the White House, but his words washed over her like a gentle waterfall. Since her first political job, she'd been on staff in one capacity or another. From campaign volunteer all the way up the ranks to communications director, she'd been Boone's protégé in all things political. She'd attended hometown rallies and national conventions. But this was her first state dinner. And she was slightly terrified. No. She was totally terrified.

Could she remember those long-ago cotillions where she'd learned place settings and greetings? Did she offer her hand or wait for the other person?

"Breathe, Georgie."

She gulped in air and fought the urge to put her head between her knees. The gown's tight skirt didn't leave room for that. "That's easy for you to say."

He patted her hands, which she realized were clenched on her lap. "When we arrive, your door will be opened and a military escort will offer his arm. Someone else will make sure your dress is lying correctly, whatever that means." He winked at her. "You'll enter with your escort and everything after that will just come naturally. Trust me."

"Ha. Just goes to show what you know!"

The limo turned onto Pennsylvania Avenue. Her breath caught as she focused again on the evening's events. Mainly, her escort tonight. Senator Clayton Barron. Panic choked off her breath once again and stars circled her head the way they did in the cartoons. Good thing she was the only one who could see them.

They were stopped by the guards at the gates, who checked their IDs and invitation. Moments later the big vehicle slid to a smooth stop in front of the East Doors. A man in an army dress blue uniform opened her door and handed her out, Boone tight on her heels.

He leaned closer and whispered in her ear, "Are you sure you want to do this?"

She whirled to face him. "You picked a fine time to ask me that, Boone Tate."

The sorry son of a gun laughed. At her. And winked, his devilish grin hinting that he was up to no good. She'd been well and truly set up. Narrowing her eyes, she muttered through pinched lips, "You are so going to pay for this, Boone."

"Smile, sugar. You'll thank me in the morning."

Breathing deeply, Georgie lifted her chin, but the army officer offered his arm before she could reply. A female air force officer appeared beside her and twitched the back of her dress into place. Georgie managed to murmur a "thank you" under her breath. Straightening her shoulders and lifting her chin—and wouldn't her mother be so proud of her now?—Georgie accepted her escort's arm and stepped toward the doors. She totally ignored Boone ducking back into the limo and the vehicle pulling away—and did it without hyperventilating.

The East Entrance foyer was full of people, but she saw Clay the moment she stepped inside. His head was bent in conversation with a stylish woman who looked vaguely familiar. One of Georgie's talents was remembering names and faces. After a mental file shuffle, she placed the woman—Ramona Morris, wife of Ambassador Charles Morris. The revelation settled her nerves somewhat. This might be a state dinner, but it was a working affair for the senator. Work. She could handle that.

Clay froze, his head raised, and turned to face her. His eyes widened and he looked as though he'd smacked face-first into a closed glass door. She'd never seen him appear dazed. Her heart fluttered and she flexed her free hand to keep from rubbing it down her thigh. Even though she wore elbow gloves, her palms were damp. Her eyes remained glued on the senator as he strode toward her.

His custom-tailored tux caressed his body in ways that made her jealous. Her palms itched, wanting and needing to touch him. One side of her brain berated her for the visceral reaction she had to him, reminding in the no-nonsense voice of her socialite mother that she was just an employee with no beauty to recommend her to a man as powerful as Clayton Barron. But the part of her that read romance novels and sniffled at chick flicks craved to touch him, to feel his hands on her, his lips on hers in a deep kiss. She remembered the question Boone had asked her. She had her answer now.

"Yes, Boone. I'm sure," she murmured, still mesmerized by the handsome man who stopped in front of her, his brown eyes hungry as he looked her up and down.

"Georgeanne."

"Senator." Was that her voice? She never sounded breathy. Ever.

"Tonight I'm just Clay."

Clay offered his arm and she slipped her hand under his left elbow. With his free hand, he tugged her fingers until they curled over his forearm and he could trap her hand close to his body. He inhaled deeply, filling his lungs with her scent. Vanilla, with a hint of something sweeter. He needed to acknowledge the army officer who'd escorted her inside but he really wanted to punch the guy. Which was ridiculous. He had no room in his life for jealousy, especially since the man was only doing his duty. Reining in the green monster, he nodded to the man and guided her toward the East Colonnade.

He didn't speak as he shepherded her along the windowed hallway overlooking the Kennedy Garden. As they approached the White House proper, two marines in full dress uniforms opened the doors. There was another long hall to navigate before they reached the diplomatic reception room, entrance there by special invitation only.

Clay entered the room with Georgie on his arm and didn't hide his smirk at the stir they caused. Years of practice kept his gait and demeanor smooth even as his heart raced. The strength of his reaction to her was totally unexpected. Though they'd worked together for years, sometimes rather intimately in hotel rooms, the confines of his family's business jet and his office, it wasn't until recently that he caught himself thinking about her in totally inappropriate ways.

He'd seen her in formal clothes before—campaign functions ran the gamut, but he'd never seen her look like… *this.* Red was definitely her color, but he'd decided that the moment he glimpsed her in the red bra and panties in his bathroom in Scottsdale. The vision, and the feel of her in his arms, had been the subject of many a dream during the nights since.

Her gown draped her curves, leaving enough to the

imagination—and his was active—to make him glad his tux jacket was buttoned. Heads bobbed in their direction, expressions curious, deferential or speculative, depending on the person. Georgie faltered a step and he tightened his arm against his side, trapping her arm. She found her footing and apologized in a soft mutter.

"What's wrong?" He'd been against this harebrained idea since Boone cooked it up. Granted, he'd planned on inviting Giselle to this soiree but after his incident of foot-in-mouth disease, escorting the star wasn't an option. Now he was worried about embarrassing Georgie. He valued her as an employee and didn't want to upset her. And honestly, he wanted her to have a good time. With him. As his date. Which was all kinds of messed up.

"Oh. Nothing. Clumsy feet."

She glanced up at him, her lashes fluttering, eyes glistening. Clay realized she wasn't wearing her glasses and a part of him kind of missed their black-framed heaviness on her face. She must be wearing contacts—and looked extremely uncomfortable doing so.

"Do you want to take the contacts out and put your glasses back on?"

Georgie swallowed a sigh. "Is it that obvious?"

"Only to me."

"No, I'll be fine." Her brow knit for a moment. "Why is that woman giving me the evil eye?"

With a casual twist of his head, Clay checked out the knot of people Georgie indicated by inclining her head their direction. In their midst stood a woman he knew well. Pearl Hudson, widow of the man whose seat Clay had taken in the senate, raised an eyebrow as she looked down her nose at Georgie.

And that pissed Clay off. Royally. While Mrs. Hudson was known as a Washington society maven, she was also known to be a complete snob. "Don't worry about her, Georgie. That's Pearl Hudson."

"Senator Hudson's widow?"

"That would be her. And she's notorious for creating scenes. There are a few people here I need to speak to so we'll just stay out of her way."

"Easy for you to say," Georgie muttered under her breath. "She's not cutting you into bite-size pieces with her eyes."

By the time dinner was announced, Georgie's feet were killing her. She managed to keep a smile on her face and not stumble through the receiving line. She managed protocol with the president and first lady, the secretary of state, and the Malaysian ambassador and his wife. She managed to sink halfway gracefully into the chair Clay held for her. She navigated dinner conversation and the place settings for the six-course dinner, all without incident.

After dessert, the guests were herded to the other end of the hall and into the East Room. A small orchestra from the navy occupied a dais at one end. Then the music started. Dancing. No one mentioned dancing. The Texas two-step was beyond her. How could she manage the waltz?

Clay took her hand, his fingers warm and strong as they wrapped around hers. "Relax, Georgie. This is the easy part."

No, no it wasn't. She'd flunked this part of charm school, branded with a big, fat F for Fail. Fairly certain the whites of her eyes were showing, she reluctantly followed him toward the dance floor. The president danced with the Malaysian ambassador's wife, while the first lady danced with the ambassador. After a few measures of music, others joined the twirling couples.

Stopping and facing her, Clay gathered her right hand in his left and placed his right hand against the small of her back. In time with the music, he stepped into her and she stumbled backward, her left hand automatically bracing against his shoulder. His right arm shifted and tightened, holding her close. He stepped again, this time to the side, then he stepped back, moving her with him.

"See? Not hard. One, two, three." He smiled and stepped forward again, forcing her back. "Right foot back, left foot to the side, right foot together. Left foot forward, right foot side, left foot together." He dipped his face toward her ear. "And remember to breathe, Georgie. That's important."

Was he laughing at her? She leaned back. He was smiling, and his eyes sparkled like cognac in leaded crystal, but he wasn't mocking her. She breathed. And relaxed. He moved her around the room, and at one point, he leaned close again. His breath ruffled the stray strand of her hair that had escaped her careful chignon.

"It's permissible to smile, too."

Georgie laughed—loudly enough that heads turned. She curled her lips between her teeth and bit down, fighting the urge to hide her face against Clay's starched shirt and tux jacket. When she looked up, he winked at her and twirled her out then back into his arms.

"See? Easy."

"When one is handsome and accomplished, of course it is."

"You think I'm handsome?"

She missed the next step but Clay was there to steady her. His expression portrayed genuine curiosity. Rather than the flippant answer hovering on the tip of her tongue, Georgie swallowed and considered. "Yes. You're handsome. When you walk into a room, people notice. *Women* notice." *I notice*, she wanted to yell.

"What makes me handsome?" Again, she caught a sense of curiosity rather than ego.

"High cheekbones. Strong jaw. Aristocratic nose. Your

hair is…" How could she tell him that her fingers itched to comb through his perfectly styled hair to mess it up and feel its thick, silky texture against her skin. She'd give almost anything to see him with bedhead. "Your hair is dark and luxurious. Rich. And your eyes. How do I explain about your eyes?"

She allowed a wry smile to tug at the corner of her mouth. "If I kept a diary, I'd describe them as cognac." *And burnt umber. Decadent as sweet toffee.*

"You keep a diary and I'm in it?"

Georgie's cheeks heated as he spun her away and back again.

"What else do you write about me?"

"No. No. I don't keep a diary."

"But I'd be in it if you did, right?"

The music ended and though Clay stopped dancing, he didn't release her. He studied her face through half-lidded eyes and Georgie shivered beneath his scrutiny. It was as if he peered into the darkest corners of her mind and if he struck a match, he'd see the secret room of a stalker. Pictures of him—snapshots of moments they'd shared, only without his knowledge or acknowledgment—lining the walls. His name traced over and over surrounded with hearts and flowers. She was so pathetic.

"Georgie?"

She stared up at him, horrified at the direction her thoughts had wandered. "I…uh…"

His cheeks creased as his grin widened. "I *am* in your diary."

Where was a desk when she needed one to bang her head on? "I don't keep a diary." Not now anyway. And thank goodness the darn thing was buried in the back of her closet in her room at her dad's house. The next time she was home she would burn that sucker.

A waiter passed by with a tray of crystal flutes filled

with sparkling champagne. She grabbed one and tossed it back like it was water. It didn't help. Clay relieved her of the glass and set it on an empty tray. "Don't look now but Mrs. Hudson is headed this direction. We should dance."

He didn't give Georgie a chance to catch her breath before he whirled her out on the dance floor. The music was slow, bluesy, and she just sort of melted into his arms. She couldn't help herself. She fit against him. Of course, the four-inch heels helped. And his broad shoulders. His arms curled around her, his strong hand held hers.

His lips brushed her forehead and hc whispered, "I think it's time we got out of here and went back to my place."

She should say no. She should call Boone to come extricate her. She should— Georgie looked up, saw a tenderness in Clay's gaze that turned her boneless. She was in so much trouble now.

Eight

The limo slid to a smooth stop beneath the East Wing portico. The same army officer from before opened the rear door. Clay handed Georgie into the backseat and ducked to follow. Hunt would be driving and he already had his instructions.

Georgie fidgeted beside him and winced.

"Problem?"

She offered him a nose squiggle and shrug. "My feet are killing me. I don't wear high heels for a reason."

There was his opening. "Why doesn't your building have an elevator?"

"It does. But…" Her cheeks flushed. "Claustrophobia?"

Now her blush made sense because his thoughts went right back to that evening in Scottsdale, too. Red was definitely her color and he wondered if her lingerie matched her dress. He fully intended to find out.

"Ah, yes. Claustrophobia and nyctophobia all in one package, tied up with a red bow."

"Go ahead. Make fun. Must be nice to be perfect."

Clay laid his head back against the buttery-soft leather seat and offered a rumbling helping of laughter with a side order of self-deprecation. "Sweet pea, I am far from perfect. Just ask my father."

"Ha. Just goes to show he doesn't know jack."

She'd muttered but he heard what she said and hid his smile. "I'm glad you have such faith in me, Georgie."

Swiveling on the seat, she faced him. Her earnestness almost created a halo around her. "I do. We all do, Clay. Don't you get it?" She took his hand without noticing she'd done so and continued gazing into his eyes. "You care. Here." She patted his chest over his heart with her free hand. "So many don't. You do things not because they're expedient or make you look good or help out some lobby group. You do things because they're the right things to do."

Georgie's hand landed on his thigh and he barely held on to his poker face. He liked the weight and heat of her touch. A lot. She looked so earnest as she continued.

"I know people want you to run for president. I think you'd be an amazing president. I'll vote for you." Her voice trailed off and she looked down. Surprise blossomed in her expression when she realized they were holding hands. She tugged but he didn't let go.

"I hear a *but* in there, Georgie."

"The senate will miss you."

The import of her words kept him silent on the rest of the drive. The car stopped in the alley behind Clay's house. Hunt exited, checked for any possible threat, then punched the code for the secured gate next to the garage while Clay helped Georgie out.

"Come inside for a nightcap." He didn't ask, but it wasn't quite an order, either.

Georgie offered him a lopsided smile and limped beside him. He chuckled—not at her discomfort but at the twists and turns their conversation had taken. How did they get from her feet hurting to his position in the senate? He glanced back over his shoulder and dismissed Hunt with a short nod. Georgie would be staying the night.

Inside, he settled her on the couch—a piece of furniture chosen for comfort far more than design. Deep, long and covered in aged "bomber-jacket" leather, it was a couch a man could nap on during a football game or could sit on and read countless bills, feet propped on the overstuffed ottoman.

"Wine?"

"I'd prefer decaf coffee. Or a Diet Coke?"

"I can handle that." He checked the fridge. No Cokes.

Time for Plan B. Microwaves heated water, right? And somewhere in the pantry was a jar of coffee. Hopefully. Rummaging, he got lucky—a box of Starbucks single-serve tube things. Vanilla latte flavor. Georgie must have left them after one of their marathon strategy sessions. He emptied one in a coffee mug, added water and stuck it in the microwave for four minutes.

While he waited, he tugged on the ends of his black tie, unraveling the bow, and popped the first two buttons on the stiff white shirt. The microwave dinged and the water was boiling when he reached in. Maybe four minutes was a little long. He found a bigger mug, poured the boiling water in and added a splash of cold water from the tap. He stopped dead. Did Georgie use cream or sugar? Did vanilla latte need extra? He had milk, if it wasn't sour. And sugar, if he could find the sugar bowl.

"Georgie? I fixed one of your Starbucks vanilla latte things. Do you need milk or sugar?"

"Thanks, but no. It's good just the way it is, Clay."

Her voice wafted in from the living room and he breathed in relief but made a note to restock his fridge and pantry. He carried the mug out and handed it to her with a caution. "It's hot."

Dropping to the ottoman, Clay reached for Georgie's feet.

"Wait! What are you—"

He slipped off one shoe and started massaging the ball of her foot, effectively cutting her off as she let out a whimpering moan that went straight to his groin. "Want me to stop?" She whimpered again, and he chuckled. "Drink your coffee, Georgie. You did me the favor of coming to the dinner tonight at the last minute. The least I can do is rub your sore feet."

"Mmmhmmm." Her eyes closed as she relaxed against the back of the couch.

Divesting her other foot of its shoe, he rubbed them both simultaneously, using his thumbs to massage the balls of her feet. He had to stop when she almost dropped her cup. Clay snagged it and set it aside then went back to work. In moments, she was all but purring. He continued for a few minutes, stopping only when she struggled to sit up.

"Keep doing that and I'll be asleep in moments."

"Can't have that happening." He shifted, lightning-fast, from ottoman to couch, gathering her onto his lap. He teased his finger around the neckline of her dress, from one shoulder across the swells of her breasts to the other shoulder, and back again.

"Clay—"

"Georgie."

"We shouldn't be doing this."

"Maybe." He buried his nose behind her ear and nibbled the soft skin he found. "Want me to stop?"

He continued to kiss her, nuzzling along her jaw to her mouth. Full lips. Soft. Sweet. Just like the woman. He deepened the kiss, waiting for her to open for him.

"Georgie?" He murmured her name against her lips.

She leaned back and stared at him, looking helpless and unsure.

"Sweet pea? What is it?"

"I've wanted this…you… I've dreamed about it…but…"

"Shhh, darlin'. This is good. We're good." And it shocked him to realize he spoke the truth. This wasn't a simple seduction. He *liked* Georgie. As a person. And was just now discovering how truly sexy she was. Coming into a relationship from this direction was a revelation. "We're more than good, Georgie."

He recognized her surrender in the way her eyes softened and went unfocused, in the way her arms crept around his neck, in the way her lips sought his and her body pressed against him. "Will you stay with me tonight, Georgie? In my bed?"

At her sighing yes, he gathered her into his arms and stood up. She gasped and her arms clutched around his shoulders and neck. "I promise not to drop you."

Her green eyes flared with something he'd never seen there before—desire. And trust. "I never thought you would."

A soft light came on as he pushed the bedroom door open. He should thank Hunt for installing the motion sensor. Clay gently lowered Georgie to her feet. Cupping her cheeks in his palms, he kissed her. He wanted to strip her and take her right there, but his practical side poked him. Once he started making love to her, he wanted no interruptions, no distractions.

"Contacts?"

She blinked up at him, bemused and dreamy. "Oh. Um…"

"Your bag?"

"Oh. Yes." She seemed to give herself a mental shake and smiled. "Yes. Case and drops."

"If you need to…ah…" He waved toward the set of French doors on one wall. "The bathroom. I'll be right back."

"Clay?"

Something in the tone of Georgie's voice stopped him dead in his tracks. "Yeah?"

"Can you…uh, will you…unzip me?"

He turned around and schooled his features. Even in the low light, her face flamed. He wanted to be the one to strip her out of that gorgeous gown, but he could see the impracticality of that. And bless Georgie, she was always practical. "I can do that." Damn. Was that gravelly rumble his voice? He swallowed hard and returned to her.

She turned her back to him and he futzed with the hook

at the top then pulled the zipper to reveal some sort of… His brain drew a blank. Red satin and lace did that to a man. Bustier. That was the word for what she wore. Oh, yeah. He could strip her out of that. It looked like a hellava lot more fun than her dress.

"Um… Clay?"

"Mmmm?"

"I…need to…uh…you know…go?"

Embarrassed, he released her. When had his hand curled around her waist? When had his mouth dropped to kiss the nape of her neck as his other hand cupped her breast? "Yeah. Me, too." He needed to go somewhere. He did his best to focus. To the living room. That was it. To get her bag. So she could take her contacts out. He pivoted and trotted out because if he stayed, he would have watched her step out of the dress, would have followed her into the bathroom like a stray dog begging for a kind word.

When he returned, she was still in the bathroom. He knocked on the door, passed her purse through when it opened a crack and retreated to his bed. Damn but he felt awkward, like a pimple-faced kid in the backseat of his daddy's Oldsmobile. Only he'd never been that kid. Ever. Not his first time, or any of the times after. Not until now.

And that was when it hit. Tonight—Georgie. This was something more, something special. She was definitely something special and he'd been an absolute idiot and blind to boot. He stripped out of his jacket, resisted the urge to rip his shirt open, scattering the studs. Instead, he studiously removed each one. Took off his cuff links. Kicked off his boots and sat to strip off his socks. He was still sitting on the edge of the bed when Georgie stepped out.

Her legs were long and muscular, with thighs rounding into her very lovely butt. Nipped-in waist, full breasts, and… Clay dragged his gaze to her eyes—blinking owlishly at him sans glasses—and hoped to hell he wasn't drooling. He stood up, suddenly needing the extra room in his slacks. He held out a hand in silent invitation.

When she arrived, stumbling a little as she walked with one hand extended as if she was afraid of bumping into something, he gathered her against him. His hands traced up her sides, smoothed down her back. Over and over. He didn't think he'd ever be able to stop touching her. Her forehead connected with the bare skin of his chest and he forced air into his lungs. Breathing had suddenly become overrated. Her fingers clutched his shirt plackets and he felt the shiver that slid through her.

He pulled the pins and clips from her hair and tunneled his fingers through it until it framed her face. The bustier she wore was unhooked and gone with nimble flicks of his fingers, and her red panties followed with the whisper of silk against skin.

"I want you, Georgie," he murmured against her hair. She nodded, her silken hair rubbing across his lips. He twitched when she kissed his chest. "Ahhh, baby," he sighed. Scooping her into his arms, he carried her to the bed and settled her toward the center. "I've wanted this since Arizona."

She blushed and looked down, almost coy in her reaction. Then her gaze met his and Clay's pulse rate tripled. The need and want on her face were as naked as she was. He climbed on the bed, still wearing his shirt and slacks, wanting only to touch and pleasure her.

Running her hands down the hard, muscular plane of his back, Georgie found the hem of his crisply starched shirt and snuck her fingers beneath. His skin felt warm, smooth, but for the feathering of hair sprinkled across his chest, which was now gently abrading hers. His muscles flexed under her touch.

She had one too-short moment to savor the sensations

of hot skin and starched linen before he pushed up and slipped his shirt off. Capturing her wrists in one large hand, he pressed them to pillows above her head. "I get to touch you first."

She might have protested, if her brain still had the ability to form words she didn't have the breath to utter. Wide-eyed, she gazed up at him, watched his mouth curve into a predatory grin, his amber eyes looking almost feral. He simply watched her, touching her only with his breath, her hips pinned by his, her wrists still shackled.

"So pretty." His expression shifted from wonder to possessiveness. "And now mine."

Clay released her wrists but she didn't move, captured in his heated gaze. He pushed away, sat back on his knees between her legs. His gaze roamed over her, as visceral a caress as if he'd stroked his palm across her skin.

She shivered uncontrollably, not from cold, but from the heat building up inside her. He made her feel hot, crazy with need, all common sense scattered into the shadows of his bedroom. Now that she had given in to the desire, all she wanted was to touch him, to feel his weight on her, to know what he felt like buried deep inside her. Only that would satisfy her now.

Georgie didn't know where her feelings came from. This eruption of desire might stem from her long-standing crush, or it could have ignited from the look in his eyes. She ached, deep inside, needing him. Wanting him as she'd never wanted anyone else. She couldn't deny her feelings any longer.

His hand, surprisingly callused, followed the path of his gaze, stroking the curve of her cheek and down over her throat. He skimmed across her collarbone and lingered at her breasts, palm cupping her, fingers gently kneading until her breath hitched, fast and uneven. He didn't hurry, giving each breast attention, treating them to touch and tweaks until she bucked beneath him.

"Shhh, Georgie. I want to take my time." He smiled, holding her gaze a moment before the warmth and weight of his body disappeared. She heard something soft hit the floor—his slacks. Clay was back in a moment and his hand continued the journey lower. Rough fingertips teased across her belly, making her quiver and reach impatiently for him. He caught her hands, banding her wrists easily, refusing to be rushed.

He pressed on the soft curve of her belly, and she waited for embarrassed heat to flush her cheeks. She'd never had a flat, trim stomach, not like the women Clay normally dated. The feeling didn't come. How could it when he watched her, his desire so evident she could read it without her glasses. Deep appreciation shone in his eyes, and she relaxed a moment before growing bold enough to push her hips against his hand, begging for his attention.

Clay obliged, caressing from one hip to the other. His fingers curled around her curves and he squeezed gently. She closed her eyes, picturing him gripping her with both hands, thrusting into her. Where did these ideas come from? Sex before Clay had been awkward fumblings in the dark. Her mind conjured images of him spreading her legs wider, his fingers sliding into that aching space between them. Her eyes flew open as his hand did just that.

Fingertips teased her, accompanied by a low hum of male appreciation. As his fingers continued their explorations, she tensed, bracing for the moment when he reached the burning need inside her. She squeezed her eyes shut as her hips tilted upward without any prompting from her. As time, in sync with her erratic breaths, skipped to a stop, she waited for…something, the moment one of exquisite torture.

It didn't come. Instead of his sliding fingers sinking

into her, they were replaced by his breath blowing across her core. Something warm and slick brushed across her, the touch unexpected but welcome. His breath came again, stirring gently against her skin before he descended to taste her with his mouth, soft and wet and hot and sending her wits scattering.

He was going to kill her. She fisted her hands in his hair—his perfectly trimmed and styled hair—and arched against him, crying out, unable to bite back the sound. She felt his smile, her moans of pleasure urging him on. He teased her, tormenting and tasting, lapping, stroking, nibbling as if she was a feast laid out for his pleasure. She was ready to beg, plead for him to finish, to push her over the edge into the storm of pleasure he'd created deep within her. Clay had no mercy. He used his mouth shamelessly, and finally his fingers—one, followed by another—curled inside her relentlessly until she shuddered, bowing her back, feet and shoulders pressing against the bed, as she went blind from the enormity of the emotions crashing over her.

As she fell back against the soft mattress, her throat burned, raw from what? Screams?

Clay didn't wait for her to recover. He crawled up her body, a predator capturing his prey. He blocked out everything as he hovered over her, braced on his hands. He lowered his head, caught her lips with his, kissed her. Her fists released the comforter and rubbed along his lean flanks, circled his back. Her fingers dug into the taut muscles and he groaned into her mouth.

She tugged him closer, wanting his weight settled on her, wanting him buried inside her, stroking in and out. She would have crawled inside his skin if she could have, but even that wouldn't have been enough. She wanted to be part of him. Needed him to be a part of her. Then his hips lifted and he grasped her hand in his.

"Touch me, Georgie. Take me in your hand and guide me inside you."

She did as he asked, savoring the hard feel of him, a tiny part of her noticing he wore a condom. He sank inside her and her breath hitched. She'd gone a long time without a lover and never had she felt so complete, so alive, as when his body joined with hers. Clay stilled, watching her, both of them savoring the power of the moment. She wanted to look away, but she couldn't, knowing he was sinking inside her soul as easily as he had her body, stretching and filling her.

She wanted to speak, wanted to tell him how good this felt, how sexy and thrilling, how completely perfect she found this moment, but she had no ability to form the words. Instead, she just whimpered and moaned and clutched at his shoulders, lifting herself up to him.

Her fingers slid up the back of his neck, fisted in his thick, black hair. She tugged to bring his head down to hers. She wanted to taste him, fill her mouth with the flavor of him. She whimpered and Clay took mercy, claiming her mouth in a desperate kiss.

Desperate—yes, that defined how she felt. Desperation colored everything, every look, every touch, every kiss. Their bodies moved to a primitive rhythm as she reached for something less physical, something more spiritual than just a climax.

His breath, moist and heated, teased against her cheek. How was he not panting, gulping in great lungfuls of air the way she was? Tension wound tighter, then Clay shifted, changed angles, and light burst in her brain. She shattered into stardust, watching as tiny sparkles of Georgie rained down on them both.

She felt as though she needed to sweep up all that shiny glitter to save in a jar so maybe—just maybe—she could put herself back together. She felt infinite, a part of the universe, transcendent and powerful. Her vision cleared and she focused on Clay's face. His features were etched with his pleasure and she clung to him as he tensed and poured himself into her. They'd each taken and then gave back to the other pleasure a thousand times more intense.

He collapsed over her, rolling to the side and wrapping his arms around her. His sweat-sheened skin pressed against the length of her body, and the lazy strokes of his hand up and down her back made her want to arch and purr like a well-satisfied house cat. Basking in the afterglow, she concentrated on the one thing she could managc without thought—breathing. As her heart slowed, the stardust that was the essence of her settled back into the bottle made up by her skin until she once again became the woman named Georgie Dreyfus.

Her brain, like her heart, slowed its madly whirling attempt to make sense of things. A thought, not even fully formed, tapped against her consciousness. Words. She should say something, but that would mean stringing syllables together to form a coherent thought. She was too tired, too incoherent for that. Words could wait.

Everything could wait. Her world may have just gone topsy-turvy, but it would still be there in the morning, waiting to be dealt with.

At least she thought it would. With her last shred of coherence, she noted that Clay kissed her forehead and murmured something that sounded like, "Sweet dreams, love."

Nine

Georgie lay very still when she remembered where she was. Beyond the windows, the city was coming awake. Traffic. Voices. The noise of life in DC, but much closer than the sounds she normally heard from her third-floor apartment. Clay's house. Clay's room. Clay's…bed. With Clay asleep beside her.

She wanted to flail. To hyperventilate. To totally freak out as warmth at her back reminded her that she'd plunged headfirst into waters way over her head. Memories of the previous night flooded through her and she fought the temptation to get up and flee. Not just run for the hills, but escape to the farthest place on earth. Totally not practical. Plus, she'd never been a quitter. Smoothing out her breathing, she cautiously turned her head.

Clay had ended up on his back, his right arm flung above his head. She lay curled on her side, her back to him, using his biceps for a pillow. His chest—his very masculine and muscular chest with its fine feathering of dark hair—rose and fell in time with his measured breaths.

She squeezed her eyes shut. *Breathe. Just breathe*, she reminded herself. Last night had been a hundred times more wonderful than anything she'd ever dreamed. And here she was, still in Clay's bed. This had to be a good thing, right? She'd overheard Hunt and other members of the security team grousing about predawn pickup and deliveries. Georgie couldn't remember Clay spending the night with anyone but Giselle. Which meant she shouldn't make more out of this than it was. A one-night stand. An anomaly. An error in judgment… No. She refused to think that. The things they'd done last night had *not* been a mistake.

"You're thinking too loudly."

Georgie startled and flipped over to stare at Clay. His warm brown eyes appeared sleepy and amused. And there was something she couldn't quite identify lurking in his gaze—something that flushed her skin and made her want to snuggle up with him under the covers.

"I didn't mean to wake you."

His mouth quirked into a smile and she really wanted to lean up to kiss his lips. Before she could act on the urge, Clay cupped her cheek and tugged her closer. Their lips met, his nibbling hers before he swiped his tongue over them, teasing until she opened her mouth. His tongue dipped between her lips to taste her and Georgie almost choked. Mortified, she pulled away and put her hand over her mouth.

Clay stared at her, clearly confused. "Sweet pea?"

"Um…mrmingbrth."

"What?"

She ducked her head and tried not to exhale when she spoke. "Morning breath."

His eyes widened slightly and then he guffawed. "Honey, I haven't exactly brushed my teeth, either." Still laughing, Clay rolled over, pinning her to the bed and kissing her soundly. Breathless, and far more aroused than she should be, Georgie pushed against his chest—ineffectually. He held her close until her arms crept around his neck and she arched closer.

Long minutes later he raised his head. "I think we need a shower. And a toothbrush." He winked and laughed at her outraged expression before kissing her again. "C'mon. Then I'll buy you coffee."

Georgie groaned. Coffee. Up until now she hadn't necessarily believed there could be life before coffee. Clay had definitely disproved that theory. "Yes. Caffeine. I needs it, my preciousssss."

Clay insisted his shower was big enough for two, and

darn if it wasn't. That built-in bench had uses Georgie had never considered. Leaving her almost too boneless to wash her hair after making love to her, Clay stepped out while she finished. It wasn't until she was out of the shower and wearing an oversize terry-cloth robe that Georgie panicked. She peeked out the door.

"Clay?"

"Mmm?"

"I don't have any clothes here. Well…except for my formal."

He flashed a grin so wicked her knees threatened to buckle. "Damn. That's too bad, sweet pea. Guess we need to head back to bed then."

"Clay!"

"Mmm?"

She threw up her hands. "Argh!"

Laughing, he disappeared into his walk-in closet. A few moments later he reappeared wearing jeans slung low on his hips and carrying something. "You'll probably have to roll up the sweatpants, but they should fit well enough. The shirt will swamp you but with one of my jackets over it, no one will notice."

"Um, can't we just go to my place so I can change?"

He waggled his brows. "You gonna wear my robe?"

"Oh. Yeah. No."

"Get dressed, Georgie."

"Yes, boss."

She snagged her panties off the floor and ducked back into the bathroom, closing the door behind her. Sinking onto the toilet, she fought the urge to put her head between her knees. No panicking. Yes, he was her boss. Bosses dated employees all the time. But he was a *senator.* And she was a senior member of his staff and…and…

Georgie gave up when she stopped breathing. Dropping her head, she forced air into her lungs. She didn't hear the door open and didn't realize Clay was there until he was kneeling in front of her.

"Sweet pea, what's wrong?"

"I...we...can't..."

"Shhh. Yes, we can. Trust me. I've had this argument for months now. We're both adults. We're both professional." He took one of her hands in his big one and cupped her cheek with his other. "I'm going to be honest here, Georgie. I don't do commitment."

Her heart sank.

"Giselle was...convenient."

Georgie pressed her lips together so Clay couldn't see them tremble and buried her free hand in the fluffy robe for the same reason.

"You aren't."

"I'm not?"

"No. You aren't convenient at all."

"Oh." This conversation was going downhill quickly.

"I want to be honest with you, Georgie."

"Ohh...kay."

"I can't promise forever. Not right now. But I'd sure like to give this a try, see what happens. I..." He rocked back to sit on his heels and removed his palm from her cheek to rub it through his messy hair. "I want to see if maybe there's a future for us. You make me want all sorts of things. I want to take care of you. Make you smile. And I damn sure want to make love to you again."

He gave her hand a little squeeze and waited for her to respond. She just sat there, staring. He wanted to date her? Her inner fangirl squeed and bounced in excitement before her brain caught up. This was wrong on so many levels, but that didn't matter. He wanted to take care of her. To explore the feelings blossoming between them. That was the message she received from his words, from the expression on his face—a face she knew so intimately because she'd studied it, working with him to add nuance to the words she wrote for him. The man was a spectacular speaker, but this was no act. *Please*, she whispered up to the universe. *Let it be real. Let this...us...be real.*

"Okay."

He arched a brow at her. "That's not exactly the reaction I was hoping for," he replied drily.

Before she stopped to think about it, she cupped his face in her palms, leaned forward and kissed him. She focused all her feelings, all the pent-up hopes and dreams of a nerdy young woman yearning for something—someone—she never thought she'd have a chance with.

When they finally broke the breathless kiss, Clay laughed softly. "Yeah, that's more like it. Now get dressed. I need coffee."

He rose and backed out, shutting the door. Georgie found her panties and pulled them on before yanking on the sweats. She had to roll the waist of the pants after tying the drawstring as tight as she could. The thing still rode low on her generous hips, but she was pretty sure they wouldn't fall off. The long-sleeved henley covered the jerry-rigged waistline.

It wasn't until she walked out that another thought hit. "Shoes." With a disgruntled curl of her lip, she added, "I can't very well wear my heels to the local coffee shop."

"Yeah, I can see how wearing those with sweats might not go over with the fashion police."

Georgie stared at him then blinked several times. "Fashion police?"

Glancing toward the ceiling, Clay exhaled deeply. "I spent way too much time around Giselle. Then again, she wouldn't be caught dead wearing my sweats."

Georgie cringed at his words and hunched her shoulders.

"Which is stupid because I think it's sexy as hell."

Well, didn't that just perk her right up. She pressed her

lips together to keep from giggling. “Well, I spend most of my life in fashion jail but I’m revolting simply because those suckers hurt my feet.”

Clay ducked out, calling over his shoulder, “Wait…”

Following him out, Georgie watched him trot downstairs and heard him rummaging around. He reappeared with a pair of rain boots in his hands.

“Aha! I thought I remembered you’d left these over here. I’ll get socks for you to wear.” He climbed the steps, tossed her the boots and headed into the bedroom.

She followed, her brows knit in consternation. “Are you sure these are mine? I don’t remember leaving them here.” In fact, she didn’t remember the boots at all.

He peered at her from the closet. “Pretty sure those are yours. The only other woman who’s been over here is Giselle and she wouldn’t be caught dead wearing those.”

Georgie’s jaw dropped. “Excuse me?” She caught the pair of socks he threw with one hand. “Why wouldn’t she?”

“Too practical. And they don’t carry a designer label.”

Clay studied her expression for a long moment then strode across the room, a second pair of socks in his hand. He dropped the socks into one of the boots and cupped his fingers over her shoulders. “Let me explain, sweet pea. Giselle is a sports car—built for speed and high maintenance. You? You’re a Ford pickup, built for comfort and long distance.” He kissed her before she could protest. “And trust me, this Oklahoma boy will come home to comfort every time. Now put your boots on. I want coffee and food. You wore me out last night.”

He disappeared downstairs before she could process what he’d said. A truck? He compared her to a truck? And called her…comfortable. Georgie sat down on the edge of the bed and pulled on his socks. He’d been smart to give her two pairs of socks. The galoshes were made to be worn over shoes. She needed the extra padding. Clomping down the stairs, she found Clay standing by the front door, holding up a jacket. She slipped her arms into the sleeves and was surprised when he dropped a kiss on the top of her head.

"I meant that as a compliment, sweet pea." He murmured the words, slipping his arms around her waist and pulling her back against him. "Don't get bent out of shape. Yes, Giselle is beautiful in her way but when it comes down to what's important? I'm picking you."

"You are?"

"I am." He turned her, his hands rubbing up and down her arms as he gazed at her. His expression was both bemused and sincere. "You've been here right under my nose and I've been too stupid to recognize what I had. Have. Because you're here. I have you. And I want to keep you."

"You do?"

Clay threw his head back and laughed. "For a woman who makes her living with words, you've become rather… reticent."

"I have?"

He kissed her forehead, turned her toward the door and gave her a nudge. "If it makes you feel any better, I'm a bit blown away by this turn of events, too."

"You are?"

"You're repeating yourself, sweet pea."

Georgie planted her feet and twisted her head to look at him. "Clay, I need to be honest here."

His eyes shuttered but he didn't interrupt her.

"I'm…this…us…" She inhaled, held her breath and exhaled, but her hands still shook as she turned and reached out to touch his chest. "I've had a crush…"

"I know, Georgie."

"You do?"

"Well, I know now. I guess Boone saw it all along. He was just waiting for me to pull my head out and realize what a treasure you are. Professionally, yes, I knew that, but I have the feeling that—" He snapped his jaw shut and his eyes cut away from her.

"What feeling, Clay?"

"You're real, Georgie. And I find myself needing a whole lot of that—of you—in my life. Is this forever? I don't know. We've just started this—" He gestured between them with his hand. "Whatever this is. I care about you. As a friend and now as something…more. I can't make promises to you. Not yet. But damn if I don't want to give this my best shot."

Everything she'd wished for and then some was standing right here in front of her. All she had to do was acknowledge her feelings. She stretched up on her toes and placed a gentle kiss on his lips. "Me, too."

Clay exhaled on a relieved laugh. "Can we go eat now?"

Feeling lighter and happier than she had in ages, she preceded him out the door. As they exited the security gate separating his yard from the sidewalk, Georgie looked up and recoiled, stumbling backward. Clay caught her in his arms and held her steady.

"Well, well, well. Look who we have here."

Ten

They'd been ambushed by Parker Grace. With a catty smile, the reporter drawled, "Fancy meeting the two of you coming out of the senator's home the morning after you appear together at a state dinner. Lovely sweats you have on, Georgeanne, but then you've never been known for your fashion sense."

Georgie needed to remember to be careful what she wished for. She wanted to scream at the top of her lungs. Caught red-handed by the one woman who could create a maelstrom in the press and more problems for Clay's up-coming presidential bid than Georgie could shake a stick at. Her mind spun like slick tires in a mud pit. She had no response, no story spin to give the nosy reporter to make this look like something other than it was. Before her brain could engage, Clay squeezed her arm.

"Reduced to skulking now, Parker?"

The woman glared at him, a portrait of righteous indig-nation. "No. I just happened to be walking past."

Her excuse was flimsy and they all knew it. Georgie opened her mouth to explain away her presence, but Clay's hand gripped her shoulder. "Well, I'll make it easy for you, Parker. Georgie and I are headed to the Daily Grind for coffee and muffins. No, you aren't invited to join us. But if you hurry, you might be able to get a cameraman over there to catch two colleagues sipping coffee and stuffing blueberry muffins into our mouths."

Without waiting for a reply, Clay urged Georgie away, hand now on her back. At the end of the block, Georgie glanced over her shoulder. Parker, cell phone glued to her ear, stared after them.

"You shouldn't encourage her."

"Probably not." Clay pulled her to a stop and gazed at her. She blinked up at him owlishly. "Where are your glasses?"

She shrugged and dug the toe of her boot into the sidewalk. "I didn't have room for them in this." She pulled out the ridiculously small beaded bag Jen had loaned her.

"Can you see anything?"

"Sure." Her gaze shifted sideways. "Well, sort of. Up close anyway."

"Good. You'll have to rely on me." He didn't even try to hide thc pleased grin. "Now, about Parker. It's rather fun to jerk her chain."

"She's a shark, Clay."

"Not even close. A barracuda maybe. A small one." He started walking and tugged Georgie along with him. "Are you embarrassed to be seen with me?"

Now it was her turn to stop and tug him back. "Are you serious? I'd think it was the other way around!"

He arched a brow, daring her to continue. She sputtered for a moment, flustered.

"I am serious, Georgie. I thought I'd made myself clear on this point. I want to date you."

Her face blanched and she gulped in air.

"Breathe, Georgie. I don't have a paper bag."

"Will. Not. Hyperventilate."

"Good. Look, I don't want to stress you out, but you know me. Once I make up my mind, I don't do things halfway." Her snorting giggle brought him up short.

"Clay, other than Giselle, you've never dated the same woman longer than a month."

"Well, that's true. But none of them were you."

He wanted to laugh when she sucked in a breath, beyond flustered now. Instead, he pulled her against his chest and rubbed his hands down her back. "As far as you and I are concerned, my name is officially out of the dating pool,

Georgie. At least while we are committed to this relationship. We'll take things a day at a time."

"But…the campaign. And…and…"

"And what? You are an intelligent, articulate and very sexy woman." That statement got another giggle and snort as she pushed away and glanced down at her baggy sweats. *His* baggy sweats, and didn't it just turn him on that she was wearing his clothes? Maybe he should call to have food delivered so he could take Georgie back to bed. Then his stomach rumbled. He would ensure his fridge and cabinets were stocked from now on, though, so every morning they woke up at his place, they could have breakfast in bed.

They continued walking for a couple of blocks, neither speaking. On the sidewalk outside the coffee shop, Clay halted and faced Georgie. "We'll work around things if someone discovers we have a relationship beyond work. Okay?"

Her eyes glittered as she nodded slowly. "Are you sure? I mean, plausible deniability—"

Clay silenced her with a finger over her lips. "Stop. Right there. If this leaks, I don't want to hide you, Georgie. That's not who I am." He dropped his hand and waited. This was make-or-break for him. If their relationship became common knowledge, he refused to skulk in shadows. In his position, hiding anything from the press or the public was a bad idea. Part of him wanted to throw caution to the wind, but the practical, political side counseled discretion. As Georgie had said, "Plausible deniability."

"Are you with me, Georgie?"

A smile struggled to form on her face as she squared her shoulders. "Yes, Clay."

"Good. Now I'm starved and if my brain doesn't get caffeine soon, it's going on strike." He pulled the heavy glass door open and ushered her into the softly lit shop.

Once they were seated at a table for two near the front

windows, Clay studied her, noting how she fidgeted and looked everywhere but at him. If he had less ego, he might be worried, but he had two advantages. He was a Barron and he knew Georgie. She edged toward reticence but she wasn't afraid to speak up in defense of an idea. They'd had some passionate debates over the years and to see her flustered was a real treat. This meant he'd gotten to her. He still had some reservations, despite Boone's pushing, yet sitting here with Georgie felt right.

As a rule, he considered the consequences before making a move, and this whole thing felt reckless. Yet after spending the night with Georgie, he wondered why it had taken him so long to realize what Boone had known all along. Georgie was perfect for him. Smart, politically savvy, sweet in a charmingly real way and fantastic in bed. Oh, yes, they were definitely compatible in that regard. He should have guessed given her fire when they discussed the issues.

As he watched, she pulled out her phone and read the screen. Her thumbs flew as she texted back. A stab of jealousy twisted in his gut. The ping of his own phone distracted him. He tapped the accept call button and put the phone to his ear.

"Where are you?"

"Good morning, Boone. Nice of you to call."

"Ycah, whatever. Where are you? And where's Georgie?"

"We're at the Daily Grind."

"We'll be there in a few minutes."

"Ah, no you won't."

"Hunt and I will pick you up. Please tell me Georgie isn't still wearing her gown."

"She's not. She's wearing a set of my sweats."

"Your…oh."

Silence stretched a little longer than Clay would have liked.

"So, last night…"

"Why are you calling, Boone?"

"Something's up. Besides you, I mean."

Clay groaned at his cousin's bad pun, but Boone rushed on before Clay could reply.

"Trust me. We need face time. After we pick y'all up, we'll swing by Georgie's apartment so she can change."

"What's up?"

"This is an all-hands-on-deck situation. I promise."

"Fine. See you in a few."

Clay asked the barista to change their order to go and grabbed the drink carrier and bag when she passed it over. At the table, Georgie was still madly texting. He cleared his throat to get her attention and she glanced up, looking guilty.

"Boone and Hunt are picking us up out front."

"Oh." Her head jerked, and her gaze latched onto his. "Wait. What?"

"Something's come up. C'mon."

She pushed back from the table, stood and followed him out the door. The black SUV slid to a stop at the curb about a minute later. Boone jumped out to open the back passenger door. Georgie slid in. Then Clay handed her the drinks and bag containing their muffins and climbed in. A moment later, Boone was in the front seat and Hunt pulled smoothly into traffic, despite the honking behind them.

Georgie turned to look and laughed. "Well, that was close. Parker took your advice. That was a camera crew from WTDC honking at us."

She swiveled to face the front, but the humor in her expression died as Boone stared back, worry etched on his face. Clay glanced from his cousin to Georgie and back. "Okay, cuz. We're face-to-face. What's up?"

"Cyrus."

His father's name dropped into a pool of silence and Clay's stomach clenched. "What's he done now?"

"He filed the paperwork for a PAC."

Clay wasn't too surprised, given the conversation the old man had forced on him at both Thanksgiving and Christmas. "So? It's not exactly a secret that I'll be seeking the party's nomination."

"He's hired you a—" Boone coughed into his hand. "Dream team."

Georgie leaned forward, her lips pursed and brow furrowed. "He hired handlers?"

"Yup."

Not waiting for the other shoe to drop, Clay pushed. "What else, Boone? You wouldn't be wasting your Sunday morning if there wasn't more."

"Cyrus wants to fire me and Georgie. And announce your engagement."

Georgie squeaked, her eyes wide and shocked as she pivoted in her seat to nail Clay with a look. "Our *engagement*? But…last night was our fir—"

Boone cut her off. "To Giselle."

Hunt dropped them off in front of Georgie's apartment and went in search of a parking space. Boone followed them up the stairs, which irritated Clay no end. "We don't need a chaperone."

"Yeah, I'd say that horse is already out of the barn, cuz. This isn't chaperoning, this is strategizing."

Inside her apartment, Georgie left the men in the living room while she ducked into her bedroom to change clothes. First, though, she settled her familiar black-framed glasses on her nose. Being able to see clearly was a gift. Too bad it was only her eyesight that was fixed and not her heart and brain.

Her cheeks heated at the thought of her gaffe earlier.

How could she have thought Clay would jump from a one-night stand into an engagement with her, her girlish fantasies notwithstanding?

Gathering her wits and a huge helping of intestinal fortitude, Georgie emerged to face the three men waiting for her return. Boone lounged on her couch, as if he planned to take an afternoon nap. Hunt had snagged a chair from her kitchen table and sat straddling it, his arms crossed over the back. Clay occupied her reading chair, feet propped on her ottoman. She grabbed another chair but Clay moved his feet and patted the ottoman.

"Sit here, sweet pea."

Just as she sat, her front door burst open and Jen stood there, her gaze flicking over all of them as she processed the scene. "Georgie? The senator's in your chair."

Hunt pushed up from his chair and ducked behind her best friend to shut the door, twisting the dead bolt this time.

"Jen! What are you doing here?"

"You didn't come home last night," the other woman accused. "I came down to get the juicy details." She waggled her brows.

Georgie wanted to pretend this wasn't happening. Instead, she watched Hunt extend his hand.

"Hunter Tate, Clay's director of security."

Jen glanced at Hunt, and then Georgie watched her friend's whole body react. She looked him up and down as she offered her hand. "Jennifer Antonelli. Georgie's best friend."

Her eyes cut to Boone. "Wait. Tate? Are you and Boone related?"

"Brothers."

"Holy cannoli. Are there more of you at home?"

Georgie giggled, unable to hide her amusement. "Honey, the Barrons and Tates are known for throwing sons."

"I have no clue what that means, but I think I've died

and gone to that big romancelandia buffet in the sky." She sank onto the chair Hunt had vacated, a dreamy look suffusing her face.

"It means there are five Barron brothers and…" Georgie counted on her fingers.

"Seven Tates," Boone finished for her.

Jen's mouth gaped before she screeched, "Wait. Wait! OMG! Is Deacon Tate your brother?"

Georgie pressed her lips together to keep from laughing at the look of disgust Boone and Hunt exchanged over the top of Jen's head.

"Never heard of him," Boone muttered.

She sensed Clay's silent laughter as his palm skimmed down her back. The practical angel on one shoulder cautioned her about diving into water over her head. The devil on the other side insisted she needed to take a running jump into the deep end.

Clay continued to surreptitiously pet her as he spoke up. "So what are we going to do about Cyrus?"

Eleven

Monday morning Clay arrived early at the office. He and Georgie had dodged any mention in the news cycles for Saturday and Sunday, despite Parker nosing around. He didn't expect to find his father sitting in his office.

"Who is this?" Cyrus stabbed at a blurry photo on the front page of a tabloid more likely to feature a Photoshopped picture of a Hollywood starlet and Bigfoot above the fold.

The corners of Clay's mouth curled down in a perplexed frown. "Good question."

The old man rattled the paper. "You know who it is, Clayton. You broke up with Giselle for this woman?"

"No, I can't tell who that is or when that photo was taken. And get out of my chair, Dad." When his father didn't move, Clay shrugged. "Fine. Sit there all damn day. I have work to do."

Snagging some files from his in-box, Clay pivoted and headed for the exit.

"Don't turn your back on me, Clayton."

When the desk chair squeaked, Clay turned around. "Don't order me around, especially in my own office." He pointed to one of the leather armchairs arranged in front of his antique mahogany desk. Very little occupied the desk's surface—his in-box, a telephone console, his nameplate and an antique bankers lamp with a green shade and patina-dark brass base.

Clay waited until Cyrus settled into the guest chair before he rounded his desk to sink into the worn leather seat. The files landed on the desktop. "First, I stopped seeing Giselle before Christmas, though to be precise, she broke off things with me. I won't call it a breakup as no actual relationship existed between us. She was convenient. That worked both ways."

"You need to fix it, boy. You're declaring for the presidency in a few weeks. You need a woman next to you who looks good. Giselle will make a fine first lady."

"What part of *I'm not seeing Giselle any longer* do you not understand, old man? I'm done with her."

"And I'm saying you aren't. Nobody is going to vote for a bachelor for president. Time you got with the program, boy. That doesn't include this woman." He glowered at Clay. "I know she writes your speeches. Women like her are a dime a dozen. Get her out of your system, fire her ass and then get back with Giselle."

Cyrus surged to his feet and went to the door. "I've rented space for the election team, but you need to clear out space here in your office so they can work closely with you. That woman is going to be trouble. I could see it when you brought her home. Get shed of her. My people will be ready to move into her space by the end of the week."

The door closed behind his father's back but Clay didn't move. When the door opened again, he glanced up, angry and ready to let his father know. Boone stood there, arms folded across his chest as he leaned against the doorjamb.

"So Plan A didn't work."

Clay huffed out a frustrated breath then chuckled. "Actually, it went exactly according to plan."

Friday morning dawned gray and rainy. Thursday night Clay and Boone had flown to New York for a meeting with some campaign finance bundlers. For the first time in a week, Georgie spent the night in her own bed. Alone. And she discovered she didn't like it, not one little bit. How could she have gotten so used to sleeping with Clay—she who never spent the night with anyone, not even as a kid on a sleepover?

His gentle snore, the warm solidity of his body curled around hers, the kiss he greeted her with in the morning, and if they had time, some wake-up sex. Georgie now had a whole new appreciation for wake-up sex. And shared showers. And drinking coffee sitting at the breakfast bar in Clay's kitchen.

"We are in sooo much trouble," she told her reflection in the mirror.

Racing through her morning routine, she was out the door, travel cup in her hand, and headed for the Metro well before her normal time. With fewer commuters to contend with, she arrived at the office almost an hour early. The security guard at the door greeted her with a smile as she folded her umbrella. With a wink, she passed him a vanilla chai from the coffee shop next to the Metro station, where she'd gotten a refill before walking to the building.

The door to Clay's office wasn't locked and she wondered if Evelyn, his secretary, had also come in early. None of the other staff had keys.

"Ev, it's just me."

No one answered her greeting. Moving cautiously, she headed deeper into the warren of offices. Maybe the "boys" had come back early. Ev's desk, situated just outside Clay's office, was empty and showed no signs of being recently occupied. His door was closed and locked, with no light showing beneath it. The hair on the back of her neck prickled as she crept down the hallway. Boone's office, next to Clay's, was also devoid of life. She heard a loud thump and muttered curse. The sounds came from her office, through the partially opened door. *Her* office should have been locked, too.

Georgie pulled out her phone and scrolled to the number for the senate security office. Her thumb hovered over the call button as she peeked through the door.

A man in a well-tailored business suit was pulling things

off the shelves in her bookcase. He was in his midthirties and nice-looking in a slick, Madison Avenue way. A woman, a bit older, also in an expensive black power suit, stood behind her desk emptying every personal item on her credenza into a box.

Georgie hit Call, her presence announced when she spoke into her phone. "This is Georgeanne Dreyfus. There are intruders in Senator Barron's office. I need security code red."

The couple paused and exchanged a look. Then they looked her up and down. The man's expression turned speculative while the woman dismissed her out of hand with a curled lip and a sniff.

"Why are *you* here?" the woman asked, obviously the one in charge.

"This is my office. I'll ask the questions."

"No, this is my office. You've been fired. You were supposed to be cleared out by now so I could move in."

"Fired?"

"Yes, fired. As in your services are no longer required, what with the senator running for president and all. Mr. Barron assured us that we'd have access starting today."

"*Mr.* Barron? The senator's father?"

"Is there another Mr. Barron?" The woman looked at Georgie as if she was a total idiot.

"I don't work for Mr. Barron. I work for the senator."

A male voice called from the reception area, "Miss Dreyfus?"

"Back here, officer."

Her friend from the front door and another guard appeared. "You got a problem, ma'am?"

"I do, yes. I am Sylvia Camden." The woman spoke before Georgie could. "I'm in charge of the senator's campaign. This woman has been fired. We are packing up her personal items to make sure she takes nothing of a proprietary nature with her. You will stand by until we are done so you can escort her from the premises."

Georgie felt her mouth drop open and her eyes widen at the woman's audacity.

"Ms. Dreyfus?" The guard looked uncertain now.

Punching her phone again, she called Boone, making sure the call was on speaker.

"Hey, sugar. What's up?"

"Boone, is the senator nearby?"

"Sittin' across the table from me havin' breakfast. Why?"

"Would you put me on speaker? You both need to hear this."

"Georgie?" Clay's voice washed over her and she had to remember to breathe.

"Sorry to interrupt your meal, sir, but we have a situation at the office."

"What's wrong?" His voice sharpened.

The woman strode up next to Georgie and in a strident voice announced, "Senator Barron, I'm Sylvia Camden, your campaign adviser. This woman has been fired and we're clearing out her office."

"Georgie, do you have security there?"

"Yes, two officers."

"Good. Then they can hear me. Ms. Camden does not work for me. She is to be escorted from the building and banned."

Georgie heard the anger seething in Clay's voice as he continued. "I'll say this one time, Ms. Camden. Georgie works for me. My entire staff works for me. Not my father. You, on the other hand, do work for my father. Not me. Now get out of my office and do not come back."

"Senator—" Camden attempted to cut him off, but he didn't allow it.

"Georgie, have security escort her out. I want a report

made to the capitol police for trespassing, breaking and entering, and vandalism."

Boone's voice followed on the heels of Clay's. "How'd they get in and not set off alarms?"

"The door was unlocked." Georgie eyed the woman. "How did you get a key?"

"I told you. I'm the senator's campaign advi—"

Clay's irritated voice blasted from Georgie's phone. "I don't *have* a campaign adviser, Ms. Camden. Therefore, you do not work for me."

"Sir, I work for your father."

"Georgie, make sure security retrieves any keys. And find out who gave them access."

"Yes, sir!" She shouldn't feel so gleeful but Georgie wanted to do a little Snoopy dance standing right there in the hall.

"I'll be back in Washington by early afternoon. We'll discuss this situation then."

"Yes, sir."

"Take your phone off speaker, Georgie." Clay's voice warmed and she hastened to follow his order, holding the phone to her ear and backing away from the door so the two guards could get inside.

"Yes, sir?"

"I'm sorry, sweet pea. My old man is a piece of work, as you are well aware. I'll deal with him. Inventory everything they touched. If there's so much as a smudge, he'll pay for it."

"Okay."

"Call for reservations at Max's. I'll buy you a steak then take you home and make it up to you for having to deal with the old man's crap."

"Okay."

"Bring an overnight bag, sweet pea. In fact, we need to talk about you leaving some things at my house so you don't have to run back and forth to your place when you're staying with me."

Her strangled voice choked on the word so it came out breathless. "Okay."

"I'll see you around one."

"Okay."

She hung up, dazed and feeling like an idiot. Okay? That's all she could get out of her mouth when the man she had such intense feelings for informed her that he wanted her to move some of her things into his house?

"Georgie!"

She jumped and stared at the petite woman who ruled Clay's office, his long-time secretary and administrative assistant.

"Ev?"

"Hon, I've been saying your name for nearly five minutes. You wanna tell me why security hustled those two people out of here?"

The warm, glowy feeling generated by Clay's words faded beneath the harsh reality of the past thirty minutes. "That woman and her assistant came from Mr. Barron."

"Oh, Lordy, hon. Say no more. When's the senator coming back to town?"

"This afternoon."

"Yup. Figured he'd be cutting this trip short. Did she tell you that you were fired?"

"Yes."

"That old jackass is up to his tricks again." Ev patted her shoulder. "Don't you worry, Georgie. The old coot has fired me more times than I can remember. I'll find out how they got clearance and keys."

The phone on Georgie's desk rang. "That's my cue to get to work."

Clay lathered shaving cream on his cheeks, watching Georgie through the mirror. She lay sprawled on her stomach in his bed—their bed now. He hadn't convinced her to actually move in with him, but over the last few weeks, some of her things were slowly migrating into his closet and onto the counters of the vanity in the bathroom. He *liked* having her in his house. A lot. And that was like taking a kick from a mule. There was no getting used to things, no need to make concessions to having her underfoot all the time. He preferred her with him. The nights she spent at her own place left him restless and pissed off.

He continued to feel off balance though he had a better understanding of his brothers' predicaments now. Cord and Chance both found the women who completed them. He'd never considered finding his own. Was Georgie the one? Or was this some idiotic infatuation that would cause him to crash and burn—personally and politically?

"Okay, how's this sound?" Georgie cleared her throat as he turned to face her, offering her his entire focus. "My name is Clayton Barron. Some of you are familiar with my name. By the time this election is over, the entire country will know who I am." She glanced up from her notes. "A little too arrogant?"

"Keep going."

"Okay." She coughed into her hand and pushed her glasses up to the bridge of her nose. "The Office of the President of the United States should be held by an individual who has actual solutions to change America for the better. We need to fix the things that are broken. We need to remember the principles upon which America was founded. This country needs a drastic new approach before it's too late. Change is never easy, but if we do things as they've always been done, America will stagnate even more.

"If you're sitting here tonight, it means you have questions and want answers. You're here because you care, because you want to know what I plan to do. You want to make sure I have real solutions to the problems that matter—the economy, national security, the ability of future generations to fully embrace the freedoms past generations have fought and died for. No one can truly be free without economic security. No one can truly be free when our enemies threaten our very existence."

Georgie pushed up, shifting her body so she was sitting cross-legged on the bed. "Ugh. It sucks. Totally and completely."

"It doesn't totally and completely suck."

"But it sucks." She sighed loudly, grabbed her hair and twisted it on top of her head. Jabbing her pen into the messy bun, she made a show of ripping up the top sheet of the yellow legal pad. "Maybe your father is right. Maybe you do need that team he keeps trying to shove down your throat."

She looked so thoroughly disheartened and sad he wanted to wrap her up in his arms and assure her everything would be okay. He grabbed a washcloth and wiped the shaving cream off his face so he could do just that. Joining her on the bed, he pulled the pen from her hair so it cascaded around her shoulders. He loved the silken fall of it, loved the way it played through his fingers when he kissed her, which he did at that moment.

"Love your hair down," he murmured. Leaning in, he teased her bottom lip, nipping lightly before claiming her mouth. "What's wrong, sweet pea?"

"Nothing."

"Georgie."

She sighed and leaned against his shoulder. "I hate doctors."

He furrowed his brow, trying to follow her non sequitur.

"My yearly checkup is this morning at ten," she explained.

He zeroed in on her mouth again, this time using his tongue instead of his teeth. After a long moment he put enough space between them that he could see her face. “It’s just a physical, honey.”

“Guys have it easy,” she groused.

Only then did he understand. This wasn’t just a yearly physical, this was a yearly…exam. “Oh.”

Georgie nodded solemnly. “*Oh* is right.”

“Want me to go with you?”

Blushing furiously, she shoved at his shoulder and scrambled away. “Ewww. No! Nada. Nyet. Nope.” Then she laughed. “Thanks for the offer, but I’m a big girl and the tabloids would have a field day if they caught us together at my ob-gyn’s office.”

“Good point.”

“I get first dibs on the shower.”

“I have a better idea. Let’s save water.” He waggled his brows, rolled off the bed and scooped her into his arms, losing his towel along the way.

The shower was hot and steamy, which had nothing to do with the water temperature and everything to do with tongues and hands. Afterward, Clay dried Georgie off and sent her to get dressed with a pat on her very sweet, heart-shaped behind while he finally finished shaving. He had a meeting with that blasted election team so he could get them out of his hair. He didn’t need or want them and he’d counted on Georgie—and Boone—to be there, to show they were a team. Still, he couldn’t begrudge her the time for this appointment. He needed to take a page from his younger brothers and put his foot down where his father was concerned. He didn’t need backup for that. He could handle the old man. And he would. Or else.

Twelve

Had it only been a month? Georgie peeked out the curtains of Clay's townhouse, frowning at the throng of photographers swarming the sidewalk outside his gate. She texted Hunt with the situation and received a reply that a car would pick them up in the alley behind Clay's garage.

The story had snowballed after the blurry picture of them appeared in that tabloid after the state dinner, and Parker Grace had led the charge. Talk about the poster child for Women Scorned Anonymous. Even now, Parker was camped outside with a cameraman.

Clay jogged down the stairs and cocked his head. "Georgie?"

"We have to go out the back. Hunt's bringing a car."

"I take it the herd is restless?"

She rolled her eyes. "That's an understatement." Sighing, she peeked out again and turned back to face the man who'd become her everything—and needed to become her nothing ASAP. She rubbed her fisted hand across her chest over her heart, surprised at how much the decision she'd come to this morning—after a solid week of harassment—hurt.

Clay's expression sharpened and he stepped closer, arms reaching for her. "Sweet pea?"

Despair washed over her and Georgie threw up her hands to keep him from touching her. "Listen to me, Clay. I care for you, but I care even more *about* you. I'm still your communications director, which means I'm your employee. That dang reporter outed us and look what's happened. We can't go anywhere together without getting hounded. You're the front-runner for the nomination, even without a formal declaration. You will be the next President of the United States. We can't play at being...a...a thing any longer."

"A *thing*?" Clay's voice dropped into the bass range, his displeasure evident in his tone and expression. "This is no game, Georgie, and our relationship is not a *thing*."

Her heart fluttered at his intensity. Clay Barron had a reputation on the Hill—most eligible bachelor. She'd seen the women he dated. This…*thing* between them was only a fling. It had to be. Even if walking away broke her heart.

She wasn't the right woman for him. She wasn't a starlet, supermodel or debutante. She was plain ol' Georgie Dreyfus with drab brown hair, thick glasses and muddy green eyes.

Clay grabbed her shoulders and gave her a gentle shake, the careful action totally at odds with the stormy expression on his face. "I'm not going away, Georgie. This is something real. At least to me."

His gaze searched her face, probing all the way into the place she hid her deepest secrets—especially her feelings for her boss. She swallowed and fought the urge to fall into his arms. "This won't work. *We* won't work."

Clay stared at her, his expression smoothing to that of the polished politician. "Oh…?"

He pinned her with his gaze, waiting for a reply. She blinked several times and ignored the ding on her phone. Clay didn't. He lifted her hand and removed her phone. He read the text and replied.

"Hunt's two blocks away."

"Oh. Right. Time to go."

The corners of his mouth curled up but the smile wasn't friendly. "This conversation isn't over. And we are far from done."

Before she could recoil, he had her wrapped in his arms and pressed against his chest. "I say when we're done. You got that?"

"But…why me? How can you be with someone like me?"

"Ah, sweet pea." His voice mellowed as he stroked her

back. "Why wouldn't I be? You're sweet and funny and warm. You're beautiful. And the best damn speechwriter on the Hill." His eyes twinkled as he said that last bit. "So. Are we clear, sweet pea?"

She blinked up at him. "About what?"

"About us not being done. A real thing. Yeah?"

"Oh, yeah."

"Kiss me, darlin'."

"I can do that."

"So why aren't you?"

"Oh, yeah."

Clay laughed and cupped her face so he could kiss her deeply. He only released her mouth when her phone dinged again.

"Time to go."

"Uh-huh."

Clay helped her into the backseat of the SUV then urged her to scoot over so he could join her. She didn't stop blushing until the vehicle rolled to a stop in front of the Russell Senate Office Building. A gaggle of reporters surged forward. Glen was out of the SUV before Hunt put it in Park, but he didn't open the rear door.

"Slide over, Georgie. I go out first." Clay tugged on her hand as he maneuvered in the tight space. She did as she was told without comment. "And I'll do the talking." At that, her expression cleared and her mouth opened. He took advantage and kissed her, his tongue sweeping through her open lips. With reluctance, he broke off. "Yes, you're my communications director, but in this instance, I'm doing the talking. You with me?"

"I…yes. Of course."

"Good. Now, big smile for the cameras." He winked and nodded to Hunt, who opened the driver's door and stepped out. Seconds later Glen opened the back door and Clay emerged onto the sidewalk. He met the barrage of shouted questions and whir of cameras with a smile firmly fixed in place. Then he moved away just enough to give Georgie space to come out of the SUV. He offered his arm, with elbow crooked, and she accepted his offer after a moment's hesitation. Her slim fingers slipped between his arm and side, curling over his forearm.

"So you two *are* dating, Senator!"

It wasn't a question so Clay ignored it. Glen moved to Georgie's side, protecting her from the press of reporters.

"Senator Barron, is it true you're forming an exploratory committee with an eye on the presidency?"

He flashed his patented Barron smile with its hint of dimple toward the reporter. "No. I am not forming a committee." He paused, waited two beats and his voice penetrated the shouted follow-up questions. "I've already formed it."

That statement was like throwing a two-ton boulder into a small pond. Ripples ran out in concentric circles and the crowd was shocked silent—for about ten seconds. Ten seconds that were long enough for Clay, Georgie and Glen to make it into the building. The reporters would have to go through security checks to enter, giving them time to escape into the elevator and up to Clay's office.

In the elevator, Glen kept his expression neutral as he faced the doors, his back to Clay and Georgie. Clay could feel the waves of curiosity wafting from her, but she didn't say a word. Every staffer knew the elevators and stairwells contained security cameras. The trip to the second floor was quick and as the elevator doors slid open, Glen stepped out, on guard and alert. Only after he scanned both directions in the hallway did he motion them out.

Clay and Georgie were ensconced in his office, the door shut with Ev and the rest of his staff on the other side, before Georgie spoke.

"You've already formed an exploratory committee?"

Did she sound hurt? Clay reached for her and led her to his couch. He sat down but had to tug her hand to get her to join him. “Yes.”

“Oh.”

Yeah, definitely hurt feelings. “Sweet pea? Look at me.” When she didn’t, he cupped her cheek and pressed until her head turned. “And that committee has nothing to do with those idiots my father hired. You, Boone, Hunt and a few other people I trust, including my brothers, comprise the committee.”

“Me?” Her voice quivered slightly.

“Of course, you. You’re my communications director.” He leaned closer and dropped a soft kiss on her mouth. “And more. I trust you, Georgie. And I value your opinion. I did even before we…” He trailed off without finishing. After another gentle kiss, he added, “Before we became involved.”

“Oh.”

“Yeah, oh. I’m not doing anything without consulting the people I trust, and you’re right there at the top, Georgeanne. Okay?”

When she smiled, her eyes lit up and Clay realized he liked being the one to put that expression on her face. Off balance at the idea, he shelved it. Things were happening too fast to stop and consider why. Later. He’d deal with his emotions later.

Thirteen

Georgie couldn't breathe and her vision was fuzzy around the edges. Pushing through the heavy glass doors of her doctor's office, she walked blindly down the street. No. No, no, no. This wasn't happening. When the nurse had called two days ago to say she needed to come in to discuss the results of one of her tests, Georgie figured it had to do with her blood sugar—her dad was diabetic—or her blood pressure. A lump in her breast had been what she least expected. Today the doctor had performed a biopsy and was sending the tissue off for further tests. She kept walking, head down, fighting tears.

"Ms. Dreyfus? Ms. Dreyfus!"

She ignored the urgent voice calling to her. She didn't know where she was going, what she was doing. This. Could. Not. Be. Happening.

"Ms. Dreyfus. Georgie!" Glen grabbed her arm and tugged her to a gentle stop. "Georgie, the car's back this way."

She looked at him and wondered for a moment who he was. Then she remembered. She nodded, numb and barely breathing. "Glen. I-I'm sorry. I-I got distracted."

"Hey, are you okay?"

"I… Yeah. I'm fine. I'm…fine."

Her bodyguard was still holding her arm as he led her back to the SUV parked at the curb. He settled her into the front passenger seat and buckled her seat belt when she made no move to do so. She watched him pass in front of the vehicle, his phone to his ear.

As they pulled up in front of the Russell Building, Hunt was waiting on the sidewalk. He opened her door and helped her out.

"Georgie? What happened?"

Finally emerging from her fog, she focused on him. "I'm fine. Really. Just. Fine."

"You don't look fine, hon. I'm gonna have Glen take you home."

She felt the blood drain from her face. "No. I…no, Hunt. Please. I'm fine. Really. I have too much to do today. I… Clay's speech for this weekend. And…stuff. Yes. I have stuff to do. Okay?"

"Okay, hon. C'mon. Let's go up to the office."

Ten minutes later Ev stood in the door of Georgie's office, arms folded across her chest, her expression one of concern. She stepped inside, closed the door and leaned against it. "Talk to me, Georgie. Whatever this is, we can fix it. You don't have to go through it alone."

Only then did Georgie manage to figure out why everyone was so freaked out. "No! Oh, spittin' sunflower seeds, no. I'm not pregnant!" She blurted out the denial.

Ev's arms relaxed and she let out an audible sigh as she crossed the patterned rug to sink into one of the chairs arranged before the desk.

Georgie soldiered on. "I…there were some…anomalies on one of my yearly tests."

Ev leaned forward, her concern evident. "Which one?"

She swallowed hard, her gaze skittering across Ev's face. "My doctor…did a biopsy today."

"Oh, honey." Ev scooted closer to the desk and reached over to clasp Georgie's hands. "It's scary, especially as young as you are. Is there a history in your family?"

Shaking her head, Georgie worked to control the tears swimming in her eyes. "No. It's so crazy. My dad's diabetic, but that's it. That's the only skeleton in my health closet."

"There's a good chance the biopsy will be benign, Georgie."

"I know. The doctor kept saying he was doing this out of

an abundance of caution. It'll be fine. Women my age…it's rare. That's what he said. And it's just a lump. That's all."

Ev squeezed her fisted hands again. "Have you told Clay?"

Panic surged through her. "No. Oh, good gravy, no. I can't tell him." Georgie twisted her hands to clasp Ev's. "You can't tell him, either. You…you know about his mother, right? About what happened to her?"

The older woman nodded. "Yes, hon. I've known Clay and the family for ages. She waited too late to get treatment for her breast cancer. His old man was a bastard about it. Clay nursed her until the end, and then raised his brothers."

"Then you understand why we can't tell him. Oh, please, Ev. He can't know. It's just a precaution. The results will come back negative and everything will be back to normal. His focus is the campaign. Not me." Her words tumbled over each other. "Okay? Promise me."

"I won't tell him. I suppose there's no need to worry him if this is a false alarm."

"Right. Exactly. You know him. He will worry. There's no need. I'm fine. Really."

The woman studied her for a long moment. "But I think you're wrong. I think he'd want to know so he can help you through this. That's the kind of man he is, Georgie."

She swallowed the saliva filling her mouth and hugged her arms around her stomach. "He's perfect, Ev. Too perfect for me. I…won't make him worry."

The day dragged interminably. Clay was on the Hill all day for a series of committee meetings and a session in the Senate chambers. By the time he arrived at her apartment to pick her up for dinner, Georgie had settled her nerves and had an unshakable poker face in place. She forced gaiety into her voice and plastered on a smile. Luckily, two other couples—supporters from home—accompanied them to dinner, and Georgie kept the focus on them and Clay. She was good at her job and she worked their guests hard to divert Clay's attention. Yet she caught his concerned looks. He knew her. Knew something was off.

After dinner and a long visit over coffee and dessert, the other couples said good-night on the sidewalk in front of the restaurant. Clay snagged her hand and tugged her along with him. "Let's walk for a bit."

She did not want to walk. She did not want to talk. Georgie had every intention of getting Clay home and in bed where she could keep him so distracted he forgot to ask her what was going on. The man was far too astute for her own good, especially now. With reluctance, she followed his lead.

"You going to talk to me?"

"'Bout what?" She feigned innocence, hoping her poker face hadn't cracked.

"Sweet pea, Hunt is family. You're family. We look after each other. What happened with the doctor today?" His voice held a hint of sharpness.

She answered quickly, without looking at him. "Nothing."

"Georgie..."

"Nothing, Clay. Just follow-ups on some tests he ran."

"Which tests?"

He was *not* going to let it go. She scrambled for an answer. "You know my dad is diabetic, right?"

"Yes."

"The doctor just wanted to confirm my results." There. Not exactly a lie, just a misdirection.

"You sure that's all?"

She controlled her expression and smiled up at him. "You know how I feel about sweets and pastry, Clay."

That brought out a deep chuckle and he squeezed her hand. "Point taken."

They walked a few blocks in companionable silence, enjoying the balmy spring night. Georgie recognized Glen leaning against the black SUV parked at the curb ahead of them.

Clay stopped and pulled her around to face him, his arms sliding around her waist. "Look at me, sweet pea." She tilted her head up. "You'd tell me if something was wrong, yeah?"

The expression on his face tugged at her heart. He was so protective and he was a "fixer." She didn't want to worry him. Ever. But especially now. "Yeah, Clay. If something was wrong, I would."

He leaned down and brushed his lips across hers. "Good. Let's go home, sweet pea. I want to make love to my woman."

Georgie's cell phone slipped from her numb fingers and she stared toward the door. For a week she'd been pretending everything was fine—convinced it would be—and she'd finally relaxed. They were gearing up for the big presentation when Clay would officially announce he was running for president. It would be a huge multimedia deal with appearances by his cousin, country music star Deacon Tate, a video presentation and the announcement speech.

But the call she'd just received slammed her world to a screeching halt. Her doctor wanted to see her ASAP. He wanted to refer her to an oncologist. And she'd asked for one in Oklahoma.

She had to go home. The ranch. Her dad. Home. She needed her roots, needed the red dirt of western Oklahoma caking her boots, the smell of hay and horses.

She called her dad. He wanted to know if Clay was coming with her. Clay. Oh, God, she couldn't tell him. She wouldn't put him through this.

"No, Daddy. It's just me comin'," she whispered and ended the call.

She typed out her resignation letter, remembered she'd have to buy a plane ticket. She so rarely flew commercial. She stayed in her office, the door closed and locked, informing her staff and Ev that she was working on Clay's speech and didn't want to be disturbed. Going online, she made a reservation to fly home. She reread her resignation, tore it up and wrote the letter ten more times before she gave up and handwrote a simple message.

Clay, we have to stop things now. We both know deep down we won't work. You deserve so much more than I can ever be. You deserve a beautiful woman by your side who will be the perfect first lady when you win. I'm sorry. I never meant to hurt you. I'll only hurt you worse if I stay. Please don't try to contact me.

She couldn't write the last three words her heart screamed she add. If she admitted how much she loved him, he'd never let her go. She didn't bother blotting the tears that smeared the ink. She sealed the letter in an envelope and wrote Clay's name on its face.

Her letter to Boone was infinitely easier.

Dear Boone,
I'm sorry. I'm quitting. Someday I'll explain. Forgive me for leaving you in the lurch.
Georgie

Georgie waited until Ev was on her break. She slipped into Clay's office and left both envelopes in the center of his desk. Back in her office, she boxed up a few of the most personal mementos. Boone would pack and ship the rest to her later if she asked. And she would. Eventually. First, she had to get out of the building, to her apartment, pack and head to the airport before 10:00 p.m. She was acutely aware of the passage of time. She had to get gone ASAP. Ev left early on Thursdays. Clay and Boone were on the Hill. She had to go now to have any chance of escaping.

Georgie closed the door to her office, but her fingers froze on the aged brass knob. She leaned her forehead against the solid wood. This place had been a huge part of her life. Her hopes. Dreams. But not anymore. Sounds of the senator's office hummed behind her. Phones rang. People chattered. Everything was so normal. Clay's office would run just fine without her. Clay would be just fine without her. In fact, he'd be better off.

"What's with the box, Georgie?"

She stiffened, heart pounding. Boone wasn't supposed to be in the office. If he was here, Clay couldn't be far behind. She had to get away. She'd fall apart if she saw Clay. Her goodbye letter, left in the center of his desk, would explain what she couldn't speak out loud to the man she loved.

"Just taking some personal effects home, Boone."

Warm fingers turned her around. "Sugar, you never could play poker with me. What's goin' on?"

Boone wasn't only her boss, he was also a friend. "I'm resigning. Going home to Oklahoma."

"You can't."

"Please don't make this harder. Clay's going to be the next president. I can't stand in his way."

"What the hell are you talkin' about?"

"My letter. It explains. He'll understand." Georgie turned to flee.

Boone stopped her. "No, he won't, Georgie. He loves you, even if he's too stubborn to admit it."

"That's impossible. We're impossible."

"You'll never know if it would work if you don't stay and fight for it."

"I can't. I'm dying."

Her words shocked him and he dropped his hand. She ran, tears streaming, heart breaking. It had to be this way.

Reaching the elevators, she stabbed the button repeatedly. Nothing. Fearing Boone would chase her down, she pivoted toward the stairwell. She managed four strides before Boone caught her arm.

"Whoa there, Georgie. You don't drop a word like *dying* into the conversation and then take off." His grip on her biceps remained gentle but firm, and he marched her toward an empty conference room. Once they were alone, he still didn't release her. "Now, what the hell is going on with you?"

"I told you. I quit."

"Because you're dying? You look pretty damn healthy to me, girl."

Her anger leached away and her shoulders drooped. "I have breast cancer, Boone. I'm going home for treatment."

Boone released her arm and slumped against the wall. "Ah, hell, sugar. How long have you known?"

"I…"

"Your appointment last week. The one Hunt said upset you."

She nodded. "I had a biopsy. The doctor called this morning to confirm."

"Does Clay know?"

She couldn't meet Boone's eyes. She was taking the coward's way out, but she couldn't face Clay, couldn't face the pity in his gaze, wouldn't survive his inevitable rejection. "No."

"You can't quit, sugar. You need the insurance."

"I…" She hadn't thought of that. Her only thought had been getting away from Clay before he told her to go away.

"And no offense, Georgie, but you're selling Clay short. You're important to him."

The door eased open behind them and the man himself

stuck his head in. "Something you two want to tell me?" He wore a wry smile, but the humor did not reach his eyes.

"That's my cue to skedaddle." Boone gave her shoulder a squeeze, took the box away from her and as he passed Clay, murmured, "Just listen, then do the right thing." He slipped through the door, closing it behind him.

"Georgie?"

She forced air into her lungs but couldn't meet his eye. "I…I quit."

"I see." His voice sounded as if it had been flash frozen.

"Boone wouldn't let me."

"Ah."

"I…" She turned away from him and dropped into the nearest chair, bending to cover her face with her hands. "You know I had a checkup a few weeks ago, Clay."

"And?"

How could one word sound so brittle? "And there was a lump." She looked up at his quick intake of breath, but he wore an expression she couldn't decipher. Her gaze dropped again. "The results from the biopsy weren't…good." More silence. She continued staring at the floor.

"Prognosis?"

"Stage three. I'm being referred to an oncologist for a lumpectomy and chemo, maybe radiation. I…want to go home, Clay. To Dad's ranch."

"Okay. Give me a few days to clear my schedule. We'll go home. Get the best oncologist in the state."

Georgie didn't want to do this, but she had no choice. She couldn't allow Clay to go with her. She was too aware of what he'd gone through with his mother. That part of his life had been glossed over in his official biography—how she'd died of breast cancer when he was a boy—but Georgie *knew* him, had overheard his interactions with his brothers and his cousins. He'd been profoundly affected by his mother's illness and death. She would not put him through it again.

"You have to stay here."

A guffaw erupted from him. She had no other way to describe the sound that blasted from his mouth. The problem was his eyes held no humor. "No."

"Clay, don't make this harder—" She pushed out of the chair.

"What part of *no* do you not understand, Georgie? You aren't leaving me."

She flattened her mouth into what she hoped was a grim line, fisted her hands on her hips and attempted to mimic her mother's best society maven voice. "Now you listen to me, Clayton Barron. You're an important man." Her right hand lifted without her conscious instruction, and her index finger pointed at him, wagging in time with each word she said. "Running for President of the United States. You don't have time to be hanging around watching me lose my hair."

Inhaling so she'd have enough breath to launch into her next argument, she never got the chance. Clay stepped into her space, cupped her cheeks in his palms and leaned down until his eyes were on the same level as hers. "Now you listen to me, Georgeanne Ruth Dreyfus."

Wait? He knew her middle name? His warm breath washed over her skin and she focused on his mouth. Full lips. Square chin. Strong jaw shadowed with a day's growth of whiskers. Which only made him look far sexier than he had a right to, given the circumstances. She wet her lips, felt her nostrils flare as his cologne wafted between them—almond, cedar, bergamot and a hint of lemon. His hands dropped to her shoulders before caressing her arms as he tugged her against him. Her head fitted against his shoulder and she relaxed against his muscular chest.

"I'm not going anywhere, Georgie. I'm staying right here next to you."

"But—" Whatever argument she intended to make fled from her brain as he captured her mouth in a soft kiss. By the time he was finished, she was breathless.

"No buts, sweet pea. I'm not going anywhere. Neither of us is."

She pushed against his chest to get a little traction and pointed her finger again. Before she could poke him with it, he captured its tip in his mouth, kissing away her defenses and defeating her offense in the process.

"Clay—"

"Georgie."

He mumbled around her finger, but his eyes twinkled and a smile curled the corners of his mouth. Dang but she loved his mouth. When he kissed her, she forgot everything. All her good intentions, all her talking points, all sense of propriety. She pulled her finger from between his lips and curled it into her palm in self-defense. With his next words, the fight left her.

"I won't let you go through this alone so you might as well stop pushing me away." He dropped a kiss on her forehead. "I'm bigger, far more stubborn, and you mean too much to me."

Georgie gave up, raising her chin to glare at him. "Fine. Just...fine." Then her breath caught as the import of his words struck her. She meant something to him?

"Wait. What?"

"You heard me. I'm here to stay."

Fourteen

Clay smoothed out the crumpled paper even though the words were branded into his memory. He knew why Georgie panicked. He knew why she wanted to run that afternoon, thinking she was doing it for him. Still, it pissed him right the hell off that she thought she needed to protect him, or that he would just walk away from her.

Not gonna happen. He wasn't his father.

A soft knock on the back door of his townhouse interrupted his reverie. He pushed off the bar stool and unlocked the door. Hunt and Boone walked in, the expressions on their faces grim.

"How's she doin'?" Boone sounded gruff, but concern radiated from him.

"She's asleep."

Hunt nodded. "Good. I have a team packing up her apartment. We'll put the furniture in storage, ship the nonessentials to her dad. Clothes and personal stuff will be delivered here."

"Clay, have you discussed this with her?" Boone's voice held a note of caution.

"No. I want her here with me. End of discussion." Damn straight he wanted her here, now that he was beginning to consider his feelings for Georgie. He couldn't think about the future. He could only think about now. Maybe tomorrow at the most. Stage three. Not stage four. Not a death sentence, but three was bad enough. He shook thoughts of his mother away. If they didn't have a lifetime, then he'd squeeze every second he could into what time they had, but he couldn't think about that future. He didn't explain. His cousins remembered, too. "What about Oklahoma City, Boone?"

"We did some scrambling, but we have the Chesapeake Energy Arena locked in. Chase's media team says no problem on the change. They're familiar with the venue for concerts and that's basically what your announcement is. Deke says he'll be there with the band. They're working on a new song for your campaign. Video people will splice it in as soon as Deke sends the audio file. The advance team will have the place filled. With Deke and the Sons of Nashville leading the way, that'll be easy." Boone's gaze flicked to the wrinkled paper on the breakfast bar, but Clay cut him off before he could comment.

"She stays with me, Boone. And I stay with her. I don't care what that damn letter says. I refuse to let her face this alone." He didn't miss the look the brothers exchanged.

"Georgie is a woman who knows her own mind, Clay."

"I'm well aware of that, Hunt."

"And you know she's like the little sister none of us had. We're all a little protective of her."

Clay glared at both men. "And I'm not?"

"Dang, ol' son," Boone murmured. "This is real."

He didn't reply. He had nothing to say.

The three of them plotted long into the night before the cousins crashed in his guest rooms. Clay slipped into his bedroom. He stood next to the bed, watching Georgie sleep, and doing his best to breathe around the knot in his chest. He was not his father. He would fight for the life of the woman he cared about. He did care, knowing that's all he was capable of. At the moment, loving her—loving anyone—seemed beyond him.

Her handwritten words had shredded his gut. She believed she wasn't good enough for him. Truth was, she was too good for him. Could he make a commitment to her? Would she refuse, thinking he asked only out of a sense of obligation and pity?

Georgie stirred, her hand reaching out to the spot where he normally slept. She might try to push him away when she was awake, but sleeping? She wanted him. He stripped quickly and slipped into bed beside her, gathering her close. She breathed a little sigh and settled against him, her head nestled on his shoulder. This is where she belonged.

He was a realist. He'd watched this damn disease ravage his mother. He'd watched her hair fall out, seen her lose weight until her skin hung off her bones, her lethargy. He'd listened to his father's cruel remarks. He was not that boy anymore. He was a man—a man who would take care of his woman. No matter what.

She'd crept into his life. He'd barely noticed her that day when she appeared in the storefront campaign headquarters during his first House run. Boone knew who she was, recognized her potential. She'd been a sweet college kid with stars in her eyes. She'd worked grueling hours with no compensation. Her smile had turned shy whenever Clay spoke to her. But he'd started to notice her. She was good at what she did. And got better with experience. She worked as his state office liaison in Oklahoma City. When Boone suggested recruiting her for the DC office, he agreed immediately.

And then she was just…there. Her smile still shy when turned his way, she always managed to fit in. She *had* become the little sister the Tate boys never had. Except he'd never looked at her like that. He wasn't sure when he first noticed she was definitely *not* a little sister, but a woman with curves and green eyes that twinkled with mischief and humor. Over the years she worked in his office, he'd come to admire her talents—as a speechwriter and in the deft way she handled the media. He also realized she hid behind her black glasses, boxy suits and messy buns.

He appreciated her talents, and as he'd reminded Boone that long-ago morning in Scottsdale, he didn't paddle in his own work pool. Until Georgie had taken the brunt of the attack by those protesters. Until she'd curled into his arms as he carried her up to his suite. Until she'd laughed and cried in the dark, sharing her fears with him.

Yeah, Georgie was his now and he would not let her go.

She moved beside him, murmuring his name.

"Shhh, darlin'. Go back to sleep."

"S'everything okay?"

"I have you in my arms, sweet pea. We're good."

He felt her smile against his chest as he dropped a kiss on the top of her head. "Sleep, Georgie. We'll deal with tomorrow when it comes. Sweet dreams."

"Love you," she mumbled, unaware of what she said.

He lay awake, thinking about her words, before finally falling asleep just as the sun rose.

Boone and Hunt were sitting at the breakfast bar drinking coffee, a laptop open between them, when Clay shuffled in. He'd left Georgie sleeping, her lashes not hiding the deep shadows under her eyes. How had he not noticed how worn out and worried she'd been? Yes, she'd hidden her concern from him, but he should have realized something was more wrong than she let on. He wouldn't make that mistake again. He poured a cup of coffee and settled on a stool across the bar from his cousins.

Boone opened the conversation, but he didn't quite meet Clay's gaze. "The office knows we won't be in today."

"What now?"

Boone swiveled the computer, but before he could hit the play button, Clay's cell phone rang, the words *Chase calling* flashing on the screen.

"You're up early," he stated with no preamble as he stabbed the speaker icon.

"Haven't been to bed yet." His younger brother was constantly in the tabloids. Head of Barron Entertainment, he flitted from Las Vegas to LA to Nashville. “But I’m not calling about me.”

“Oh?”

“Yeah, I’m calling to say thanks. For once you’re the headline in the grocery checkout instead of me.”

Cold anger washed through him. “What are you talking about, Chase?”

“You haven’t even announced yet and the media is all over you like cheese and jalapeños on nachos. But seriously, Clay, why did you break up with Giselle? She was perfect for you. I know you like strays, but Georgeanne? Though I guess it makes sense, since she works for you. You and Boone need to come up with a strategy.”

Before he could respond, Boone snatched the phone. “Chase, you need to shut up.”

“Boone?”

“I’m tellin’ ya, cuz, shut it. Now.”

Silence filled the kitchen. They heard Chase take a deep breath. “Damn. Are they really a thing?”

Boone stared at Clay. An angry tic beneath one eye and the grim line of his lips conveyed his feelings so perfectly that Boone added, “You idiot. You’re damn lucky you aren’t standing here where Clay can put hands on you.”

“The old man is gonna blow a gasket.”

“He already has.”

“No, Boone. He hasn’t called for an intervention. He might be pissed, but his brain hasn’t exploded.” A ping sounded from Chase’s end and then silence. Another quick breath and then a string of cuss words dribbled from Clay’s phone. “Not yet, but any minute now. Have y’all seen the latest news report?”

“Hunt and I have, but Clay hasn’t.”

Clay stared at Boone, his gaze shifting to Hunt before dropping to the laptop. “What?”

Boone hit Play and a video featuring a perky blonde reporter flickered on the screen, the words *Political Ploy or Play for Pity?* on a screen behind her.

"Oklahoma Senator Clayton Barron has long been Capitol Hill's most eligible bachelor. In recent months he's taken himself off the dating carousel, and his communications director, Georgeanne Dreyfus, is his constant companion. The senator broke off his long-term affair with Broadway star and fellow Oklahoman, Giselle Richards. Within days Senator Barron was seen about town with the bespectacled Dreyfus on his arm. One wonders why a man of the senator's… stature—" the female reporter stopped to waggle her brows and smirk into the camera "—would lower his standards to date his mousy employee. While known for her political savvy and ability to divert the media, Dreyfus is not the senator's typical type. We've learned from an unnamed source that Dreyfus is moving into the senator's Georgetown house. Rumors have also surfaced of numerous visits to Washington ob-gyn Dr. Mike Lane, which makes one speculate as to the reason. Another unnamed source suggests it isn't a pregnancy scare, but a medical diagnosis. Senator Barron and his party have been accused of being soft on women's issues. Is this a ploy on the part of a smart politician about to announce his campaign for the presidency? Or is a desperate woman hoping the handsome senator will take pity on her as she attempts to hitch her star to his?"

The reporter turned wide eyes to the camera, but Clay didn't listen to the rest of her drivel. He slammed the laptop shut and launched his coffee cup simultaneously. The ceramic mug hit the expensive glass-tile backsplash above the double stainless-steel sink and shattered.

Chase, voice soft and chastised, reclaimed Clay's attention. "Talk to me, Clay."

"She has breast cancer, Chase. Stage three. We're coming home next week for my announcement. I'll run my campaign from there while she undergoes treatment."

More cuss words streamed from the phone before Chase inhaled. "I'm sorry, Clay. Truly. I wouldn't wish this on anyone but especially not someone close to you."

"I care about her, Chase."

"Call Cord and Chance. They need to know. All of it. And I'm sorry for being a smart-ass."

Clay caught the relieved glance his cousins exchanged. His phone buzzed, indicating another incoming call. "Thanks, Chase. Will do." He swiped his finger to end the call and checked to see who else was on the line. Cord.

"Hey, little bro."

"Jeez, Clay, are you okay?"

"No."

"How's Georgie?"

"Scared."

"What's going on?"

Clay inhaled and then said the hateful words. "She has breast cancer."

"Ah, hell, ol' son. What's the plan?"

And this was when Clay truly appreciated his brothers. At least the next two in line. The twins sometimes swam in the jerk pool but Cord and Chance always had his back. "We're coming home next week."

"The announcement still on for Friday?"

"Yes. Boone wrangled the Peake. Deke is on board."

"We'll be there to show the colors, bud. Listen, Chance is here with me. Cassie and Jolie, too. We want to know what you need, what we can do to help."

Clay's throat clogged and his eyes burned. "You just did it, Cord. All of you."

Cord and Jolie, the mother of Cord's child, had recently married. She was an ER nurse and spoke up. "If Georgie has any questions, Clay, or needs anything at all, tell her to call me. I'll be there with her each step of the way. Tell her that, 'kay?"

"Thanks, hon. I will."

"Clay?"

He swiveled on the stool to find a disheveled Georgie standing in the doorway. Her hair was mussed, one strap of her tank hovered on the point of her shoulder ready to fall off and her cotton sleep pants rode low on her curvy hips. She blinked at Hunt and Boone, her expression confused. Her cell phone rested in the palm she stretched toward him. "Why are there movers at my apartment?"

Fifteen

Clay exchanged looks with Boone while Hunt glanced out the window.

"Clay?" Georgie's voice sounded small and a little lost.

"C'mere, sweet pea." He reached out and she moved into his arms. Glancing at her phone, he realized the call was still live. "Who're ya talking to?"

She gazed up at him, looking sleepy and confused. "Jen. She says people are in my apartment."

Hunt snatched the phone and moved away, speaking softly to Georgie's best friend. Clay kissed her forehead. "I figured you didn't want to hassle with closing down your apartment, sweetheart. Hunt arranged to have some of his crew pack up your things. We'll put your furniture in storage. Most of your personal items will get shipped to your dad. The things you need every day will come here."

Her body stiffened. "Here?"

The legs of a bar stool grated against the tile floor and Boone vacated the area, snagging his brother as he walked past.

"Yeah, baby. Here. With me. I wasn't kidding, Georgie. I'm here for the long haul. You'll stay with me when we're in DC. If I'm traveling and you don't feel up to it, you can stay with your dad in Oklahoma. I've decided to move campaign headquarters to Oklahoma City. I'll work from there while you have your treatments."

"Clay—"

"Shhh, sweet pea. We'll deal with this together."

"We will?"

"Yes." He knew she loved him and warmth spread through his chest before a chill edged in. He wished he could return her love. "C'mere." He guided her to a stool then poured coffee, nudging the mug, creamer and sugar bowl toward her, along with a spoon. He splashed more coffee in his cup while she doctored her coffee.

"What's wrong, Clay?"

He studied her face. She was awake now, and coherent. Her chin rose in a stubborn tilt. She'd survived the first blow. She'd survive what he said next. He nodded, a small acknowledgment of her strength. "Hunt will be talking to your doctor's office. Someone leaked."

Color drained from her face and she swayed on the stool. He pressed the mug into her hands. "Drink, Georgie."

"There's more." It wasn't a question.

"Yeah. Drink your coffee."

Her eyes snapped and flashed in the morning light. "I don't think I want to."

He offered a wry smile. "I know you, darlin'. The caffeine will help." He breathed easier. Georgie was back. She was still emotionally bruised and he was afraid that what he was about to share would eviscerate her, but it had to be done. Then they'd take steps to stop the bleeding.

She chugged the contents of the mug, set it down on the granite counter with a sharp *tink* of ceramic on stone. Squaring her shoulders, she nodded. "Okay. I'm ready. Show me."

He opened the laptop and hit Play. Her hand groped for his, clung, squeezed. She took her glasscs off and set them aside, still listening, head bowed. His gut roiled as anger surged. When the report ended, he closed the laptop. He didn't move, unsure of how to comfort Georgie, and that left him frustrated. His instincts urged him to take her into his arms, but something held him in place. After an agonizingly long time, which was only moments according to the clock, she raised her head and put her glasses back on so she could focus on his face.

"We need to draft a statement."

"Boone will do that."

"No. We need to do it. And call a press conference." She slipped off the stool, headed to the coffeemaker and poured another cup. She returned to her seat, her expression resolute.

"You are *not* breaking up with me, Georgie."

A soft smile teased the corner of her mouth. "No, I'm not breaking up with you."

Clay leaned in and kissed her. Her knees spread to make room for him and her arms circled his chest. "Good." He whispered the word against her lips.

Georgie's cell phone rang in the other room. Boone peeked around the corner. "Not sure you want to take this one, sugar. It's CNN."

She sighed. "Let it go to voice mail. They all can." She glanced back at Clay. "When's the announcement?"

"A week from today, in Oklahoma City at The Peake."

Her lips pursed and Clay wanted to kiss them again. He could almost see the wheels turning in her head. Damn, but she turned him inside out like getting hit with a bucket of ice water followed by blazing sunshine.

Georgie pushed her glasses up. "Okay. I'll coordinate with Chase's people. We need to lock down the office here in DC. No information out, not even a *no comment*, unless it comes from you, Boone or me. Anonymous sources get cut off at the knees. For today Ev needs to put out a memo that we'll be holding a press conference Monday. There will be requests for appearances on the Tuesday morning shows. We'll see who calls after the presser. We want to answer their questions but control the supply of information."

Boone let out a soft snort followed by a chuckle. "Dang, sugar, but you make me proud."

"She's pure awesome once she gets wound up," Hunt added.

Color returned to her cheeks and a real smile curved her

lips. Warmth flooded Clay and he didn't resist the urge to kiss her this time. "Have I mentioned how much you mean to me?" He leaned back, caught the glitter of tears on her lashes. "Ah, baby."

"I'm sorry," she murmured.

Shocked, he stared at her. "For what?"

Her hand fluttered in an absentminded gesture. "For all of this."

He gripped her shoulders and gave her a gentle shake. "I'm not. Not sorry for a bit of it." That got a shocked look and a gulp. "Don't get me wrong, Georgie. What you're facing? It's killing me. I'd take it away in a heartbeat if I had the power. You'll get through this. I'll help. We'll all help."

Midday on Monday Georgie and Clay stood near the brick pad of the "Swamp Site," a spot located on the grass across the drive from the east Senate steps. A podium covered with microphones awaited them. Clay held her hand and she inhaled through her nose, exhaling through her mouth. He figured the technique was to keep her from hyperventilating. They'd worked on their statements. They were as ready as they'd ever be.

Clay gave her hand a squeeze before releasing it and stepping to the podium. "Thank you—" The high-pitched squeal of microphone feedback filled the air and people winced at the piercing noise. A sound tech ducked to the podium, fiddled with one of the microphones and slunk back into the pack of reporters and cameramen.

"Ground rules," Clay stated without preamble. "We appreciate you coming, but here's the deal. We *will* answer questions but until both Ms. Dreyfus and I have made our statements, I don't want any interruptions. We clear on that?"

Murmurs ran through the group, but no one spoke out.

"Good. First, there's been a lot of speculation about my

decisions concerning a presidential campaign. That speculation will be laid to rest this Friday, when I make an announcement in my hometown, Oklahoma City. You can check with my press office on the availability of credentials. The event will be held at Chesapeake Energy Arena. Since the OKC Thunder plays basketball there, I'm pretty sure there will be room for everyone." This elicited chuckles from the pack of reporters.

"Second, I'm here to confirm that I do have a relationship with my communications director, Georgeanne Dreyfus. We've been seeing each other exclusively for several months and haven't attempted to hide this fact. However, considering my position, innuendos and speculations have been aired freely. Now you know the truth. Yes, our relationship is serious. And that relationship is no one's business but our own."

He stretched his hand toward Georgie and she stepped closer to take it. Reeling her to his side with utmost care, he continued, "Friday morning we awoke to a report that my entire staff found offensive. That my colleagues found offensive. That my constituents found offensive." He searched the throng, found a certain reporter and met her gaze with a hard glare. He didn't smile when the people nearest her moved away, leaving her isolated. He squeezed Georgie's hand and shifted to the side, opening the microphones to her.

"As most of you know, I'm Georgeanne Dreyfus and I've been Senator Barron's communications director for the last three years. Before that I worked as his state office manager before coming to DC as his assistant press secretary and then press secretary. Most of you know me. We've talked on the phone, exchanged emails, visited in the halls of the Russell Building, at the back of Senate committee rooms and in the halls of the Capitol."

Her voice broke and Clay steeled himself to let her continue instead of taking over the microphone. All he could do was squeeze her hand to show his support. He'd wanted to be the only one speaking at this thing, but Georgie insisted she speak for herself. This was Georgie's story and she deserved to tell it.

"Thursday I received news from my doctor's office." A murmur surged through the group, but no one spoke. "I'm thirty years old and I've been diagnosed with stage three breast cancer."

Clay shifted closer to her, his arm pressed against hers as he held her hand a little tighter. She had to blink tears from her eyes and clear her throat before she could continue.

"I'm returning to my home in Oklahoma to begin treatment. This is a very difficult time for us, for Clay…for the senator and me. We would appreciate your understanding. I know he is a public figure. I know his life is a matter of a great deal of gossip and is probably infinitely entertaining. This is not funny, nor is it entertainment. This is real. It's life at its worst." She swallowed and looked at him, her gaze warm and tearstained. "I tried to quit Thursday afternoon. Senator Barron refused my resignation. Many men would have let me walk out the door, happy they dodged the bullet. Clay informed me that wasn't going to happen. He promised to walk beside me each step of the way."

She turned her head to look at the reporters. "That makes me the luckiest woman in the world."

Clay dropped her hand and pulled her into his embrace, his arms going around her as her cheek nestled against his chest. Silence enveloped the area—everyone so quiet, traffic sounds were clearly audible. There was no whir and click of cameras, no shouted questions.

Finally, one woman near the back raised her hand. Clay nodded in her direction. She had to clear her voice several times before she could get her question out. "Alexi Madison, Fox News. Our prayers to you both," she said. "Will you keep us informed of your progress? Not for the news cycle, but because we care."

He nodded, but didn't speak. A man raised his hand and Clay acknowledged him.

"David Graves, CNN. I think I can speak for all of us when I say our thoughts are with you both and we're all hoping for a swift recovery." The reporter, his expression soft, added in a gruff voice, "My wife is a survivor." When Georgie offered him a small smile in response, he continued, "I think I ask this question for everyone, Senator, given the rumors of your interest in the presidency. Will this affect your decision?"

Georgie leaned into the microphone before Clay could react. "Dave, what part of stick around for the announcement next Friday did you not understand?" This got chuckles from the group. "The senator quite clearly stated that he'll let everyone know his plans then. And no fishing for gossip in the hallways. Only four people know what he'll say and none of us will talk.

"One last question," Georgie stated as she pointed to a petite woman in the front of the group. Miriam Davis, long-time political reporter for the *Washington Post*, was known for her tough questions and bulldog devotion to digging out the truth. "Miriam?"

"Since we don't have a society reporter here, I'm just going to say this. If there's a wedding, I better have an invite."

Sixteen

They flew home Monday afternoon after the presser. Georgie's dad was at Wiley Post Airport to meet them, along with Clay's brothers, Cord and Chance, and their wives, Jolie and Cassie. After a steak dinner in the reserved back room of Cattlemen's Café, her dad kissed her cheek.

"The ranch is there when you need to come home, sweetie. You need to stay here for a while for the doctor, yeah?"

Teary-eyed, she nodded. "Can Clay and I come down this weekend? Maybe spend Saturday night?"

"Sure, baby. I'll lay in the supplies for a real ranch breakfast."

"Has Mother—" She bit off the rest of her question.

"No, Georgie. I haven't heard from her. She's in St. Tropez or someplace with that gaggle of divorcees she hangs with." His arm slipped around her shoulders as he walked her a short distance from the group. In a quiet voice, he added, "Are you sure?"

She knew exactly what he was asking. They'd shared many a conversation about Clay's romantic escapades. "I crushed on him when I was twenty, Dad. I started falling in love with him when I was twenty-five. I tripped head over heels in love with him not long after and I've stayed there ever since. Yeah, I'm sure."

"Is he?"

Georgie stretched to tiptoe so she could peek over her father's shoulders. Clay's gaze remained glued to her, his eyes warm and concerned, though his face betrayed little of his thoughts. But she knew him, knew the nuance of almost every expression. She held Clay's gaze as she replied. "I tried to run away, Dad. After I found out. I didn't want to put him through this. He wouldn't let me. He's gentle but strong and very, very stubborn. And determined to fight this battle with me."

Her lips curled into a smile she wasn't aware of until Clay returned it with one of his own. "I thought you were the only family I had, Dad." Her eyes flicked to meet his. "I was wrong. Clay is my family, too. And Boone. Hunt. Ev. Even Clay's brothers and their wives. I'm gonna be okay, Daddy. *We're* gonna be okay."

"Of course you are, Georgie. Come home Saturday. And bring your man with you."

Still on her tiptoes, she pressed a kiss to her father's weathered cheek. The man had been a rancher his entire life—working with his hands in every kind of weather southwest Oklahoma could throw at him.

Her dad dropped a kiss on her forehead. "I figure you still know the way home, girl. Call before y'all leave the city."

"I will, Daddy."

Clay approached then, offering his hand to Georgie's father. "I look forward to getting to know you better, Mr. Dreyfus."

"George, son. I figure we're gonna be stompin' around each other for a while."

When Clay's smile lit up his eyes, Georgie felt light-headed. She still couldn't believe her luck and a voice in the back of her brain urged caution. She told it to shut up and transferred from her father's embrace into Clay's.

"See you Saturday, Dad."

"We'll do burgers on the grill."

Her dad gazed at Clay for a long, tense moment, then the lines around his eyes relaxed. "Take care of my little girl, Clayton."

"Always."

An hour later Clay and his brothers were ensconced in

the media room of Clay's Heritage Hills house. Built during Oklahoma's first oil boom, the historic mansion seemed more like a museum than a home. The "boys," as Cassie referred to them, had beers and the Cardinals baseball game blaring. Cassie and Jolie had Georgie settled around the breakfast nook table, with cups of hot tea.

Jolie studied her face and Georgie forced herself to meet the other woman's gaze. Cassie and Jolie were beautiful, unlike her. Clay needed a woman like them. She pushed her glasses up her nose, breaking the staring contest. She always blinked first.

"You'll be okay," Jolie murmured, a hint of a smile transforming her expression from scrutiny to gentle concern.

"Yeah. I will."

Cassie leaned in from the other side. "What's your schedule like?"

Caught off guard, Georgie blinked at her. "My schedule?"

"Yeah. Your schedule and Clay's."

"Oh. We have to be up early to make the morning show rounds." She blanched and Jolie squeezed her hand.

"Dealing with this publicly must be hard."

"It is. But this is Clay's life. He's important." She inhaled deeply. "He'll be a fantastic president."

She didn't miss the looks the two women exchanged over her head. "What?"

"Honey, are you sure you're up to a campaign?" Cassie watched her closely.

"I don't know. It…depends."

"You know you can talk to me," Jolie interrupted. "It's been a while since I did an oncology rotation, but I can translate any medical jargon you don't understand. And Cass and I are both here for you. Miz Beth, too. You can stay with Cord and me—"

"Or Chance and me," Cass cut in.

"Whenever you have doctor appointments or treatment. I..." Jolie looked around the kitchen. "I think it would be better if you stayed with one of us instead of here alone when Clay is on the stump. I mean...oh, hon." Jolie blinked hard and swallowed. "Some of the treatments will wipe you out. You'll need someone with you."

When she could speak around the lump in her throat, Georgie's voice came out a strangled whisper. "I know. I'll... I came home so I could be with Dad. I'll stay on the ranch down at Duncan when I can't be with Clay."

"We'll drive you back and forth, then." Cassie was adamant.

"I can't ask—"

Jolie squeezed her hand. "You aren't asking. We're volunteering. We watched the press conference this morning. Good gracious. The way Clay looks at you. I've never seen him look at *anyone* that way."

"And that makes you family, Georgie. *Our* family. No way in hell you're going through this alone. *Comprende*?"

Not trusting her voice, Georgie nodded and then hugged both women. "Thank you," she whispered.

"Now, I'm thinking we girls need a spa day on Thursday to get ready for Friday's shindig. You off, Jolie?"

"Yes, ma'am. I'm off Thursday and Friday. No way am I going to miss seeing Deacon Tate on stage!"

Cassie pressed her hand to her chest and pretended to swoon. "I swear, if I'd met that man before Chance—"

"You'd do what, woman?"

Amid guilty giggles, the three women turned to face the men standing at the arched entry to the kitchen. "Chance, you know I have a major crush on your cousin."

Jolie nodded vigorously. "I second that swoon and raise you a deep feminine sigh."

The men rolled their eyes. The women laughed and pushed back from the table. Jolie and Cass hugged Georgie and winked. Cass wagged a finger at Clay. "Georgie is ours on Thursday. We're doin' the works. Mani-pedi, facials, massage and hair. Y'all work or go play golf or something."

This pronouncement elicited snorts from the men as Chance wrangled Cassie, and Cord reeled Jolie to his side. Georgie followed Clay to see them off. They stood on the porch, hand in hand, waving as the other couples departed. Georgie leaned against Clay and gave him a squeeze with the arm she had looped around his waist.

"I like your family."

"Good. Because they like you, too. At least this bunch of them."

Georgie didn't want to think about the rest of Clay's family. She figured his father despised her and she worried about his two youngest brothers. She'd watched the family dynamics for ten years, had seen how Mr. Barron played his sons against each other. In fact, she couldn't believe Cyrus hadn't already intervened. She'd been amazed when first Chance and then Cord stood up to him, threatening mutiny in the face of their love for the women they married. She glanced up at Clay and he kissed her temple, almost as if he'd read her mind.

"We can deal with whatever gets thrown at us, Georgie. Even the old man. As long as we're together. Yeah?"

She answered without hesitation. "Yeah."

Tuesday consisted of a flurry of appearances on the network morning shows, all done remotely from the various local affiliates in Oklahoma City. Hunt chauffeured them between each station, Clay holding her hand in the SUV, walking with her to the studio with his arm around her shoulders, then reclaiming her hand as they sat together for the on-camera interviews. The afternoon brought conference calls and Skype meetings with party officials in various states and a few of the campaign fund bundlers, and a follow-up with Chase's video people, all from the new campaign office opened on the ground floor of Barron Tower in downtown Oklahoma City. They worked late into the night, finally getting back to Clay's house around midnight.

They changed, climbed into bed and though Clay tried to hold her close, she rolled away, turning her back to him. Her brain was too busy, too filled with what-ifs she couldn't process.

Her first oncology appointment. Ten o'clock Wednesday morning couldn't come soon enough. Ten o'clock Wednesday morning could never come. Georgie lay stiff and staring at the shadowed wall of Clay's bedroom. He needed his sleep.

"Sweet pea?" He didn't sound sleepy at all.

She didn't reply. What was there to say? His finger traced down her spine, creating shivers in its wake. With a gentle grip on her shoulder, he rolled her to her back and propped up on one elbow, he gazed down at her. "Don't pull away, Georgie. Don't shut me out. Talk to me."

She almost snorted at that. Her girlfriends complained incessantly about how men never *talked.* How did she end up with the only one who did?

"I'm scared." The words, whispered as softly as a night breeze in a pine tree, hung in the air between them.

"Me, too."

She blinked at that then her eyelids shuttered half-closed as he leaned down to brush her lips with his. "You are?"

"Hell yeah, Georgie." He lay back down and snugged her against his side, so that her head was nestled against his shoulder. "I've finally realized how important you are to me, how much you mean to me." He kissed the spot on her forehead where the hair of her slight widow's peak met her skin. "How much I care about you. I don't want you to be sick. I don't want you to hurt. I want to make all that go away. But I can't."

His hand snagged hers where it lay on his abdomen, and he entwined their fingers. He brought their joined fists to his mouth and kissed the back of her hand before clutching it tight to his chest.

"It doesn't matter I'm a US senator. It doesn't matter how freaking much money I have. I can't make this go away with power or wealth. All I can do is hold you when you get scared. Sit beside you when you get sick."

Georgie embraced his words, wrapping them around her like her favorite childhood blanket. He cared, but he didn't love her. It would be enough. It had to be. She tilted her face up to his. "Make love to me, Clay."

He did. He touched her with hands so gentle they were almost reverent. He kissed her deeply, his tongue sweeping into her mouth. He fed on her like a man starved, peppering kisses along her jaw, under her chin. He nibbled along her collarbone, one hand cupping her breast with fingers both caressing and teasing. His glorious mouth paused at her other breast to nuzzle and suck until her back arched off the bed.

Clay continued his explorations, with mouth and hands trailing down her ribs, across her tummy, dipping low to the juncture of her thighs where he worked his magic. She squirmed, but he held her still. She moaned and he pressed closer to her, his tongue swirling, his fingers teasing. She cried his name as her whole body shuddered and a climax tore through her as hot and bright as a 4th of July skyrocket.

A breath later he was inside her, buried deep. Her thighs cushioned his hips, her heels hooked across the backs of his legs. He filled her, completed her. He pumped slowly, a gliding slide in and out that set her nerves on fire. This was a slow burn, hot embers growing in her middle.

"Faster," she breathed into his neck. "Harder."

"No," he murmured. "Not yet."

He loved her slow and easy, and then changed the rhythm so that she, at last, got what she craved. When he finally came, she came with him, and he inhaled her moans through his mouth as he kissed her. Still entwined, they settled softly back on earth from the high of their climaxes.

"Sleep, sweet pea. Tomorrow will be what it is."

Seventeen

Wednesday morning, just after dawn, she awoke in Clay's arms, head snuggled on his shoulder. His arm was around her back, hand cupping her hip as her knee rested across his thighs. She wanted to wake up this way every morning. Life would be hectic for the next year. Hectic and scary, but she felt safe here with Clay. Strong. As though she could take on the world and win—emotions both unfamiliar and appreciated. He was right. Today would be whatever it was.

After a shared shower full of kisses and touches, they dressed and drank coffee in the kitchen, sitting close to each other. She was too keyed up to eat, knowing she'd likely toss whatever was in her stomach. Clay seemed to realize this instinctively and didn't push food on her. Instead, he suggested she do her job.

"You're still my communications director, sweet pea." He winked when he said it.

As usual, Clay was right. She threw herself into work, answering emails, returning phone calls and doing what she did best—communicating. At nine Clay came into his study and closed her laptop. "Hunt's here."

Her stomach dropped to her toes. Hunt was driving them to the University of Oklahoma medical complex to meet her oncologist, Dr. Nassad. "Hey!" she groused. "I wasn't finished with that email."

"You can finish it when we get back. C'mon, sweet pea." Clay was gentle as he pulled her from the chair.

The drive didn't take nearly long enough. Filling out the paperwork in Dr. Nassad's office should have taken days. She was done in ten minutes. Clay sat next to her in the waiting room, holding her hand. He looked calm, collected, in control. She wanted to scream and run from the room. She didn't. She sat quietly, absorbing strength from the amazing man at her side.

A nurse appeared, gave instructions. Georgie was to come with her, Clay could come back to Dr. Nassad's office to wait and the doctor would meet with both of them after the exam. They parted in the hallway as the door marked Private closed behind them.

Georgie changed into a paper gown, happy she could keep her slacks on. She only removed her blouse and bra. The nurse tapped on the door, poked her head in, nodded with a small smile and disappeared. What felt like five days later—though it was probably only five minutes—Dr. Nassad knocked and entered.

He was in his late fifties, balding and fit, with a contained energy about him that filled the atmosphere with static electricity. His handshake was no-nonsense, his words blunt. Georgie liked him immediately.

After the exam he opened her files on a rolling metal stand and studied them for a long moment. When he looked up and met her gaze, she reminded herself to breathe.

"If you wish to try to save the breast, the least invasive treatment includes chemotherapy to shrink the tumors before we try a lumpectomy. If the chemo doesn't work, we'll try radiation. I want to make the tumors as small as possible before we do the surgery." The doctor watched, waiting for her response. When she simply nodded, he continued. "If that doesn't work, or it spreads again, we need to consider a mastectomy." He had a slight accent and his eyes were kind as he explained.

The doctor glanced at her file again, and when his gaze met hers, she couldn't breathe. She knew what he would say next, and to hide from his hateful words, she hid in her memory of last night. Of Clay's hands cupping her breasts, of his mouth on her, teasing her puckered nipples. She relived the warmth shooting straight to her core, the way her body responded to his touch, the way his eyes glowed with pleasure as he touched her. Could she deprive him of that? Deprive herself?

"Ms. Dreyfus, I would recommend the mastectomy now, followed by both chemo and radiation to make sure we've caught it all. Your mammogram last year was clear. This is a particularly aggressive form of cancer. You already have a new tumor forming that was small enough it didn't show on the mammogram you took last month."

No. She didn't want to hear this, didn't want to listen. She stuck mental fingers in her ears and sang la-la-las in her head.

"Ms. Dreyfus? Georgeanne?"

She refocused her gaze on him. "Not yet." Her voice croaked the words. "Last resort. Okay?"

His lips flattened out as he pressed them together. "I don't—"

"My body, Dr. Nassad."

"Yes, it is. But I think you should discuss this with your partner. I understand losing your breasts is not an easy decision, but do you wish to gamble with your life?"

"My life, too." Anger swirled around her. Why was she acting this way? Shock? Fear? Yes, both of those. But she wasn't afraid of losing her life; she was afraid of losing Clay. Yes, he'd promised to stay by her side, but after his mother's ordeal…and the way he loved her breasts? She couldn't make that decision. Not yet. Not until every last possible cure was tried.

She stared at Dr. Nassad. "We try conservative first. And not a word about this to my partner."

The doctor's disapproval was evident in his expression and body language. "I can refer you to another—"

"No. I like you, Dr. Nassad. And I trust you, even though it seems I don't. I just know that I have to try alternatives first."

"Stubborn woman."

The smile she directed toward his scowl was wistful. "Yes, sir. I am. My way first. We'll continue to discuss the outcomes, keeping all options open. Okay?"

His scowl deepened, but he nodded. "No, not okay, but we will do as you wish." He scribbled on a prescription pad and gave her further instructions before leading her to his office. He shook hands with Clay, offered more scowls directed at Georgie and shooed them out.

Their next stop was the in-hospital pharmacy where she got the drugs making up her first round of chemo. The information sheet was ten printed pages, including six listing side effects. She took her first pill before they left the hospital complex.

By dinnertime, food was the last thing on her mind. Figured. She was part of that .2% of patients who had an immediate reaction to the drug cocktail. Clay fed her ice chips and sips of ginger ale and she worried about how long he would put up with her.

"Don't go there."

She blinked at him. "Excuse me?"

"I know you, Georgie. I recognize the panic in your eyes. Not gonna happen, sweet pea. I'm with you. No matter what. Understand?"

She stared, her vision blurred by unshed tears. "Startin' to."

"Good. Now, we're going to bed. I'm going to hold you in my arms and not only tell you how beautiful you are, but show you until you get it."

Georgie stared at Cassie and Jolie. She was an only child. She could count her close girlfriends on one hand. These two women enfolded her like they were her lifelong BFFs. She'd tried to cancel their Girls' Day Out, but they showed up at the door and wouldn't take no for an answer.

Cassie put her hands on her hips, her expression stubborn. "We're headed to JJ Nails to see Jacky and Jessica because they're the best. And Tommy gives the most amazing pedicures in the metroplex. Don't argue. You need to be pampered."

Jolie looked up from reading the medical literature. "You definitely need pampering. We'll take it easy. Plus, the massage chairs are awesome! You sit and get the works while Tommy does his magic. Then, when we have pretty feet, Jacky and Jessica take over." She offered a tentative smile. "Having acrylics will help, hon. Your nails will get brittle from the chemo drugs."

"And you'll look gorgeous tomorrow standing next to Clay on stage. I got us appointments with the top three stylists at Salon Beau Monde. Because, girl, we can't look like poor relations standing next to you!" Cassie wore a huge grin even as she eased Georgie into the passenger seat of her Highlander. Jolie climbed into the backseat as Cassie jumped into the driver's.

By lunch, with glossy, French-manicured nails and toes, Georgie felt well enough to try a light lunch of homemade noodle soup and croissants at La Baguette. The afternoon consisted of discussions about highlights, haircuts and other beauty "trauma," but by the time the girls deposited her back at Clay's, Georgie's stomach had settled and the warmth of Clay's gaze as he surveyed her from head to toe made all the hassle worth it.

"Feel up to going out for dinner?"

Invigorated, she nodded. "I do."

A little grin hovered at the corner of Clay's mouth. "I kinda like the way you say that."

Flustered, Georgie blushed as Clay leaned in to kiss the tip of her nose. "Food and then bed. Tomorrow is a long day."

* * *

Friday. Day three of her drug regime and Georgie was feeling optimistic. She'd managed a real breakfast and coffee. She'd suffered through hair and makeup. She'd acquiesced to the demands of the stylist on her outfit—a softly draped dress in a muted tangerine color that she hated until she was wearing it and her makeup had been applied. The big fight came over leaving her glasses off.

"I can't see without them."

"Doesn't matter. You don't need to see. Better yet, contacts."

She glared at the stylist and managed not to stick out her tongue as Clay arrived and ended the argument by picking up the black frames and placing them on her face, followed by a mostly chaste kiss that didn't mess up her lipstick.

By the one-hour mark until airtime, the entire family had arrived. The five Barron boys looked like fashion models in suits, starched shirts and designer ties. Every one of them wore Western boots. Jolie and Cassie also wore designer duds—Cassie in a tailored pencil skirt and jacket with slight Western touches and Jolie in a crepe wrap dress with a floaty skirt. CJ chafed at the miniature suit he'd been coerced into wearing.

The Tate brothers were just as handsome when they arrived en masse with their mother, Katherine. Deacon Tate and the Sons of Nashville had been in a separate room running through the songs they planned to play when they took the stage at the thirty-minute mark.

Cyrus held court on the opposite side of the luxurious green room and Georgie did her utmost to avoid him. An occasional chill would steal over her and she'd glance over to find his malevolent glare focused on her. She could do nothing but wait for the other shoe to drop. And it would. Cyrus was getting his way with the announcement, but sooner or later, he'd come after her. A man wearing headphones around his neck and carrying an iPad ducked into the room and asked Clay and Chase to step outside.

Jolie and Cassie were sitting with their husbands, trying to keep CJ entertained and clean as he raided the buffet laid out for the VIP guests. The governor was there, along with her entourage. Several state and US legislators were there to show support—and appear on the stage behind Clay, ready to hitch their wagons to his rising star.

A wave of nausea washed over Georgie and she headed toward the bathroom, just in case. Cyrus hijacked her before shc got there.

"We need to talk," he snarled.

"No, we don't." She tried to step around him, but he cut her off.

"I'll give you five hundred thousand dollars."

Georgie rocked back and swayed, unused to the tall, skinny heels of her shoes. "Beg pardon?"

"Quit and walk away from my son. Half a million dollars."

She didn't know whether to laugh, cry or scream. "Are you serious?"

"A woman like you? It's a generous offer."

"A woman like me?" Her voice rose as adrenaline tingled all the way to her fingertips. She was vaguely aware of a flurry of movement behind her. "And what kind of woman am I?"

"You aren't worthy of Clayton. He should have stayed with Giselle. You're plain. Too plump. Those glasses are hideous. And you're just an employee. I thought I taught him better. You screw the hired help but don't move in with them. My son will be the next President of the United States and he needs a real woman at his side."

Cyrus's words felt like vicious hooks snagging into her heart and jerking. It hurt, but she was so mad, she didn't care. "Hired help? Unworthy? Real woman?" Her eyes narrowed and her mouth pursed into a snarl. She stepped into Cyrus's space and jammed her index finger into his chest, jabbing him to punctuate every point. "You listen to me, you misogynistic, dried-up old piece of manure. I've worked my butt off for your son. I've covered him with the media when you and your other sons showed up on the front pages of every tabloid in the world. I am more than *hired help* and I dang sure am *worthy* of Clay. I might not be a size three, but I don't consider some skinny model a real woman. A real woman looks like me. A real woman stands beside her man. She supports him and loves him and takes care of him." She stopped for a breath, but an arm sliding around her middle kept her from launching into part two of her tirade.

Clay hauled her up against him and she could feel his silent laughter where her back pressed against his chest. She glanced back and grew flustered when she saw his brothers standing in a half-circle behind him.

"Dang, Clay," Cord sputtered around a chuckle. "You do like 'em feisty, ol' son."

The man with the earphones stuck his head in the door. "Everyone to their places. National networks go live in five minutes."

Cyrus evidently realized they had the entire room's attention. He glared at Clay, his lips twisting into a feral snarl. "We're done here but I'm not finished with you. We'll discuss this without an audience."

It was over, for now at least. Clay entwined his fingers with hers, and then led her out toward the stage entrance. Everyone else followed. As they approached, the music of Deacon's hit song "Red Dirt Cowgirl" filled the air. The audience was singing along. The band occupied one corner of the stage, while risers covered the rest of the space. The "backdrop" people filed out while the last notes faded and the audience erupted into applause, whistles and screams.

Georgie's breath hitched. Was Cyrus right? She knew deep down she wasn't the woman Clay needed, but Clay squeezed her hand and smiled at her. "We got this, sweet pea. Yeah?"

She forced her answering smile to match his. She would not ruin this moment for him. "Yeah."

The spotlight hit them and they walked to the center of the stage while Deacon and the Sons of Nashville played the first few measures of their newest song, "Native Son," which would become Clay's campaign theme song. Clay walked to a microphone set front center stage. The audience was still going wild but calmed as the music trailed off to a soft murmur.

Clay spoke into the mic. "Hello, America. My name is Clayton Barron and I *will* be the next President of the United States."

The place erupted as music and video screens went into overdrive. Clay turned Georgie into his arms, dipped his head and kissed her, murmuring against her lips, "We're on our way, sweet pea."

Eighteen

After his speech, the music and video, after the confetti and balloons, and the cheers, life careened into the crazy zone. Clay's election team had set up a grueling schedule. He got only the weekend after his announcement with Georgie off. They went to her dad's ranch near Duncan. They ate grilled steaks and corn on the cob and charcoal baked potatoes. She slept in Clay's arms even though she shied away from doing so under her dad's roof. George just laughed and winked at Clay. And then the madness started first thing that next Monday morning.

Now, three months later, they'd been to Iowa, New Hampshire, South Carolina and more places in between. They'd appeared on morning shows, noon shows, afternoon shows from New York to Cedar Rapids to Seattle, crisscrossing the country east and west, north and south, numerous times. With many returns to the OU Medical Center for treatments. And now they were in Pittsburgh for a televised debate. His advance team was the best in the business, but Georgie remained the center of his media team. She still wrote his speeches, putting his thoughts into eloquent, heartfelt words. And the campaign process—the grueling hours, travel and constant scrutiny—was chewing her up, though it hadn't spit her out yet.

She'd grown pale, with circles under her eyes. She'd lost some weight—enough that she'd had to supplement her wardrobe to disguise that her clothes hung off her now. The doctor had changed the chemical cocktail to something far more potent. And he'd added radiation. When Clay heard her crying softly behind the bathroom door of their hotel suite, he knew the time had come.

He didn't knock, he just eased the door open. Georgie

stood staring at the hank of hair in her hand, tears streaking her ashen cheeks. "Sweet pea?"

Her green eyes met his in the mirror before dropping to her hand. "I can't do this," she whispered.

He stepped to her, wrapped his arms around her shoulders, crossing them over her chest and kissed the top of her head. "I know, love. I know. I should have sent you home sooner. Glen will fly to Oklahoma with you tomorrow. You can stay with Jolie and Cord."

She shook her head. "I want to go home, Clay. To Dad's."

"Okay, baby. Okay. That's good. Glen will be there to drive you back and forth to the city for your appointments. You can go into the campaign office when you feel up to it. The troops will love to see you."

"I'm sorry."

His eyes narrowed as he stared at their reflection. "For what?"

"For…this." She held up her hand. "For…everything."

Nothing about this situation was right. He wanted to howl in the face of the unfairness of it all. To beat his fists against the wall of gruesome reality they faced. His mother had lost her hair. His mother had turned into a shadow. And then she'd given up. He'd lost her. Cord and Chance had lost her. She'd left them alone with their father and he'd never forgiven her for that.

Clay shut down his memories and shoved steel into his spine. Georgie wasn't his mother. He'd see her through this. She wasn't a quitter. She'd fight and win. For him. For them.

"Shut up, Georgie." She blanched at his angry order. "You don't have a damn thing to apologize for." He tightened his arms and gentled his tone. "Jeez, sweet pea, you're the strongest person I know. I've watched the toll our schedule is taking on you, but I'm greedy. I want—and need—you beside me."

He inhaled and turned her in his arms so they were face-to-face. "You are beautiful and strong and intelligent and you light up my world. You don't *ever* apologize for being you, Georgie. Not to me, not to anyone. Yeah?"

A smile—an expression he hadn't seen much of lately—tugged one corner of her mouth and he bent to kiss it. "Yeah, you got it."

He kissed her again, deeper this time, with a hint of tongue teasing her lips. "Put on something comfortable, love. We're doing room service tonight."

Later, as she slept safe in his arms, Clay lay awake staring out the sheer curtains toward the Pittsburgh skyline. His phone pinged softly and he reached for it to read the text from Boone.

Plane on standby for am flight. Team set for briefing 11am. Arrive Peterson Center, U of Pitt, 6 pm. Debate goes live at 8. Georgie's tough. She'll be fine.

That last bit caused a brief smile. Clay didn't want to send her home. Not alone. Not without him. But he had to. She understood. He hit the call button on his phone and when Boone answered, he whispered instructions.

"Rearrange my schedule. I want to be in Oklahoma as much as possible and I'm damn sure going to be there whenever she has a treatment."

"Done, cuz."

And that was it. He could now settle his mind and sleep.

Two weeks later Clay was back in Oklahoma City, chafing at the delay in getting to Duncan to see Georgie. He'd arrived early that morning but the car that met him whisked him directly to Barron Tower where he was directed to the conference room for a business meeting. So here he stood.

Clay glanced at his brothers. Cord and Chance wore sympathetic expressions. Chase looked bored and Cash appeared angry, an emotion that seemed to ride his little brother harder each passing day. Their old man lounged in the chair at the far end of the table. This was new and different—and didn't bode well. Normally, Cyrus stormed in at the last minute, full of bark and belligerence.

Clay spread his feet, crossed his arms over his chest and braced for the volleys coming his way.

"What the hell, Clay?" Cash said.

He said nothing, ignoring Cash, though worry niggled at the back of his mind as he continued staring at his father. When had Cash become the old man's lap dog? Clay would have to discuss the situation with Cord and Chance when this *intervention* was over.

"You just going to stand there?" Cash pushed out of his chair and tried to intimidate him by leaning over the table. "You're weak, Clay. Weak and stupid."

"When did you learn to heel to the old man's whistle, Cash?" Chance dropped his question into the frigid silence smothering the room.

Clay still didn't acknowledge his brothers, keeping his gaze focused on his father. The tactic worked when Cyrus erupted from his chair and stalked toward him. Clay stood taller than the old man and he used that to his advantage, gazing down, expression implacable.

"You listen to me, boy. I raised you for this. I groomed you from the first breath you took to be the damn president. I hired people to take care of your announcement, to put the package together. I had your PAC organized. And what the hell did you do? Ignored everything. You spouted some idiotic nonsense that barely blipped on the polls. I'm running things, Clayton, so don't you forget it. You don't have time to be running back here like a whipped puppy. You need to be out there winnin' primary votes."

Cyrus stabbed him in the chest with his index finger and Clay fought the urge to grab it and twist.

"These are the rules. You don't fire people I hire for you. And you damn sure don't hide here at home in the middle of a campaign pantin' after that sickly, no-account woman. You're gonna be president. You better damn well act like it." Cyrus, red-faced and sputtering, jabbed him again. "You need to act like a candidate. I've hired that advance team to work the primary states for you. You should be out there pressin' the flesh, you fool. They've scheduled appearances for you every day from now until the convention. You don't have any damn time to waste on that...woman. Cut her loose. Now. We'll figure a way so it looks like she left you. That'll get you some sympathy."

Clay clenched his teeth, but didn't say anything. Was his father that crazy? Sympathy? He'd come off looking like a total jerk, not to mention that staying with Georgie was not up for debate. Loosening the fists he'd made, he didn't back away. "Here're *my* rules, old man. Don't hire people for me if you don't want them fired. I run my own campaign. I was in double digits the week after my announcement, with the package *my* team put together. I know what I'm doing."

His father cut him off. "Coulda fooled me, boy. Spendin' all your time with that woman. She's dyin', just like your mother. She's bad news and only gonna mess you up. She can't do any of her jobs—in your bed or out of it—and you're thinkin' with the wrong part of your anatomy when it comes to her." Cyrus pushed past, headed for the door. "Get rid of her, Clay. Or I will."

Disgusted, Clay headed after him, but was stopped when Cash grabbed his arm. "Don't push him on this, Clay. You won't like the consequences."

He stared at his youngest brother and his voice dropped to a menacing whisper. "Is that a threat, Cashion?" He stepped closer, until they were eye to eye. "If you, or anyone else, so much as looks at Georgie wrong—"

Cash snarled, "You're as bad as those two." He jerked

his thumb toward Cord and Chance. "Going soft over some woman. I never figured you to be this big a fool, Clay."

His fist formed and he swung before he had any conscious awareness of his action, but the forward momentum was stopped when Cord grabbed his arm and Chance pushed Cash out of range.

"Get out, Cash." Chance stared their brother down. "I don't know what bee climbed up your butt, but we're getting damn tired of it." He manhandled Cash toward the door and pushed him out. He glanced toward Chase. "You have a clue what's wrong with him?"

Chase just shook his head as Cord blew out a laugh with a wry grin. "Well, that could've been worse."

Boone appeared in the doorway and tilted his head down the corridor. "It is."

Clay stepped out in time to see Georgie disappearing into the elevator. "Did she hear?" At Boone's nod, more than a few expletives escaped. He needed to fix this.

Chance rubbed his forehead. "This is my fault. I had Glen drive Georgie up to meet you here because I thought this meeting concerned the family trust. Had no idea the old man would ambush you. Call Glen, tell him to wait so you can go after her."

Clay grabbed his phone but before he could call, Sylvia Camden appeared and snatched it.

"No time. You have to be at KWTV in twenty minutes for makeup. The interview with CBS was moved up." She tucked Clay's phone in her pocket. "She'll be fine. She's a professional. She needs some time to process. She knows how important these appearances are. Now come with me."

Boone nodded in reluctant agreement. "Glen will take her home, get her settled. You can call her later, go down tomorrow after the donor dinner tonight. You have to make this appearance, cuz. You know that."

Clay let himself be swayed. His head knew his team was

right but his heart said they were so very wrong. He cared for her. Needed her. But a part of him also admitted having her home while he was on the stump was almost a relief. That didn't make him his father. He wasn't walking away from her. She needed treatments and rest and the healing being home could bring. Things would be fine. He'd see her tomorrow, hold her in his arms and remind them both of what they meant to each other. One more day wouldn't matter. Or so he told himself.

That one more day had turned into two, and then more because the pressure of the campaign kept him away—at least that's what he'd told himself. Then he'd flown to Miami for a fund-raising dinner and Giselle was there, looking cool and elegant, and…friendly. For the paparazzi. When he saw the stories and pictures, he'd called Georgie. She didn't answer. He'd tried to call later but she'd blocked his number.

He'd finally dropped everything and come home to see her. He'd driven to her dad's ranch, found her in the barn but when he tried to kiss her hello, Georgie pulled away from him.

"Don't, Senator."

"Senator? When did we go back to being so formal, sweet pea?"

"When I realized I'm a liability and just an employee. Only I'm not even that anymore. I quit." She squared her shoulders and lifted her chin, looking at him as haughty as an English duchess. "I'm not a starry-eyed girl anymore, Senator. You remember her, right? The one who lived in your campaign office. The one who moved to DC your second term and lived on ramen noodles so she could work for you. Yeah, she's pretty much dead and gone now. So is the girl who got swept off her feet like some heroine in a romantic movie. What an idiot she was."

"Georgie—"

"Georgie what? I love you, Clay. With my whole heart. Have for ten years. I believed you. I believed *in* you. What a complete and utter fool I turned out to be. Pretty sad for someone with an IQ of a hundred and fifty-seven." She leaned against the horse she'd been brushing, her cheek resting against his arched neck as she smoothed her hand along the animal's muscled chest. "I thought we had something special. Don't get me wrong. I don't think you truly love me—you've never said the words. I'm so not your type and I'm sure not good enough to be first lady, but I thought you cared. At least a little." She sniffled and rubbed her sleeve across her nose. "You said you cared. Said you wanted to take care of me, anyway. I guess your father was right. You need a woman like Giselle. Not someone as sick as a dog who probably won't see next Christmas."

Clay didn't know what to say. This woman had always given him the words to speak. Clueless, he didn't understand why she was having a meltdown.

"Go away, Clay. You don't belong here."

He reached to touch her, but she ducked away, sliding under the horse's neck to peer at him from the other side. "Just go. I don't have the time or energy for your games, Senator."

"This isn't a game, Georgie."

She laughed, a deep, rolling burst of sound that quickly edged toward hysteria. "You're right, Senator. It's not. It's life or death. Mine. Go. You're not welcome here."

She pushed away from the horse's side and strode toward the barn's exit, leaving Clay standing flatfooted. As she slipped between the doors, she whipped off the baseball cap and the bandanna beneath it. Her once luxurious hair—the silken fall he loved to run his fingers through—was gone. Only peach fuzz remained. The potent cocktail of chemo and radiation she'd endured hoping to save her breasts had taken its toll. Just as it had with his mother.

Heat flashed through his body followed by a chill so frigid he couldn't breathe. Clay wanted to fall to his knees in the dirt and empty the contents of his stomach. Georgie didn't look back, didn't see how she'd devastated him. Instead, she marched off, head high, shoulders unbowed, her long-legged stride as graceful as a Thoroughbred racehorse's.

He watched her walk away and in that moment, Clay came to two realizations—both of which paralyzed him. He was as despicable as his old man had ever been, and he'd lost the only woman he'd ever love.

Nineteen

"So what are you going to do about it, Clay?" Cord, as always, functioned as the family's Jiminy Cricket.

Chance watched him, his expression shuttered, but anger simmered beneath his poker face. "It's been a month, Clay. She won't take calls from any of us. The girls drove down. Evidently, she was out in the barn when they got there. By the time her dad walked them down, she'd saddled up a horse and taken off. They waited all day. She didn't come back."

Clay stared at his brothers, remembering that first family intervention when everyone had ganged up on Chance, and the next when everyone but Chance had lined up against Cord. Both of his brothers had found women who loved them. Women who made them better men. In all honesty, Georgie was his touchstone. She settled him. Balanced him. Kept him centered in the crazy political storm that made up his world.

"You need to face the truth, bud," Cord chimed in.

The truth. Yes. Truth was something he'd been running from lately. He'd screwed up. Royally.

"You know who and what she is, right?" Chance's expression softened. "Because we do. She writes the words you wish you could say. She puts them in your mouth and makes not only the world believe them, but makes you believe them, too."

"She's my heart." Had he admitted that out loud? "But I'm not the man for her. I'm not good enough. Not for her." He forced down the bile burning his esophagus. "God. I don't deserve her. I…aw, hell. I didn't go after her. Not until it was too late. I ground her feelings into the dirt and then just let her walk away from me because I didn't know what to do."

Chance, ever the voice of reason—except now—gripped his shoulder. "What have you done?" His harsh voice grated in Clay's ears.

Swamped by self-loathing and helplessness, he stared at his brothers. "You saw the pictures from Miami, of Giselle kissing me?" Their expressions darkened with anger. "She was just there. For the speech. Cyrus's people set it up. Made sure of the photo op. She kissed me. I didn't kiss her back." He pushed his fingers through his hair, leaving it tousled. "And I didn't call Georgie to tell her to brace for the publicity. By the time I got around to it, she refused to talk to me, then blocked my calls."

"Dammit, Clay." Chance's curse came out as a whisper.

"That's not the worst." His brothers leaned closer. "She refused a mastectomy."

His announcement was met with silence. Chance and Cord exchanged uneasy glances before their gazes refocused on him. Chance pulled him to a chair and pushed him down to sit. A moment later they sank into their own chairs.

"Tell us."

Clay couldn't face them, despite the compassion in Chance's voice. He stared at the tips of his boots, searching for the words. Georgie. She put the words in his mouth. Always. But not this time. He inhaled and held his breath for what seemed like hours, but was only seconds. His lungs burned before he finally let the air out. He still couldn't look at them but his mouth opened and words tumbled out.

"Y'all were so little. Hell, I was only eight. One day Mom was fine and the next, it seemed like she'd faded away to nothing. The old man was never around. You know how he is. Couldn't stand to be around sickness and Mom was. Horribly, terribly sick. The doctors did a lumpectomy because the old man—" His voice broke.

Chance's expression turned harsh. "He told her she wouldn't be a woman if she had a mastectomy, right?"

Clay nodded, unable to voice the affirmative as his rage built. He swallowed around the anger and continued, his voice flat. "She tried everything. Chemo. Radiation. Homeopathic. She went to every crackpot loonytoon who hung out a sign promising a cure. She lost her hair. Her skin was paper thin and every time one of us hugged her, we left bruises."

Clay had to stop speaking, his nose and throat burning with tears he'd never been allowed to shed. Real men didn't cry, right? The gospel according to Cyrus Barron. His brothers waited as Chance placed a quiet hand on Clay's clenched fists and Cord gripped his shoulder. With their added strength, he found a way to continuc.

"I brushed her hair until it all fell out. I held her head while she puked her guts up. I begged her not to die. Not to leave me alone with the old man because I swore I'd kill him." He finally glanced up but his brothers' faces swam through a wet prism. "She made me promise to take care of you two. To love you like she couldn't anymore."

"You made sure we got to say goodbye." Cord squeezed his shoulder. "I remember her getting so thin, she looked like she was fading away. And I remember the scarves she wore."

"I remember that hideous wig. Freaked me right the hell out. I thought it was some crazy animal, alive and sitting on Mom's head." Chance lifted one shoulder in a shrug as the corner of his mouth twisted into a wry slash. "Hey, I was only four."

"Man, those scarves. I bought them with my allowance. I wanted to make her smile so I bought the most colorful ones I could lay my hands on." A dry chuckle erupted before Clay could call it back. "They were god-awful."

Chance punched his shoulder lightly. "I thought they

made her look beautiful. But then anything was better than that damn wig." He shuddered—an exaggerated move meant to bring a smile to Clay's face. It worked.

But his smile faded all too soon as reality smacked him upside the head again. "When Georgie told me? I lost it. But I never let on. She needed me. She wanted to come home so we came home."

When he ran his hand through his hair again, it was shaking. "She talked to the doctor alone. I was right there but she didn't call me in for the consult. I found out later from her dad that the doctor recommended a mastectomy. She refused it. Because of me. Because of the campaign, I guess."

"What the hell, Clay?" Cord stared at him.

"She didn't say anything beyond requesting a stop at the pharmacy for her prescriptions. But I didn't push for info. I wanted her with me. Taking pills? That meant she could travel with me. I told myself that chemo's not as bad now as it was back when Mom went through it. I wanted to believe it would work. It didn't. The radiation was harder on her. I watched her get sicker, but I didn't ask. I couldn't deal with it so I built up walls and ignored what was happening. When we were in Pittsburgh, I heard her crying, walked into the bathroom…"

He couldn't say the words, scrubbing his face with the heels of his hands instead. He hated himself, well and truly. "She was holding a hunk of her hair. I sent her home alone because I had the debate." A series of raw cuss words erupted from his mouth. "I'm as big an ass as the old man. I royally screwed up and hurt the woman that is the best part of me."

"Do you love her?"

He wasn't sure which brother asked, not that it mattered. The question was on the tip of both their tongues. He didn't even think about it. "I do. Yes."

Chance pulled out his phone and dialed a number as he stood up and walked across the room. He was the master of hushed conversations. Moments later he turned around. "You need to tell her that, Clay. Boone says she had a treatment this morning. She'll be at her dad's ranch now." When Clay didn't respond, he continued. "I'll call Cassie. We'll go with you."

Staring at his younger brother, Clay wasn't sure he'd heard Chance correctly. "We?"

Cord nodded. "You don't think we'd let you do this alone, do you? Jolie and I are coming, too."

Chance hauled Clay to his feet and hugged him tightly. "Family, Clay. The Barrons might be dysfunctional as hell, but we're learning."

He couldn't speak, the lump in his throat tight and burning. Family. How in hell had his brothers figured it out when he'd been so clueless? He clung to Chance and felt Cord's arms wrap around them both.

"You were there for us, Clay, when we were growing up. You diverted the old man's attention and we owe you for that at the very least. Most of all, you're our brother and we love you. We'll get through this. All of us together."

He blinked back tears and focused on Cord's face. His brother's expression radiated determination. And compassion. What Clay said next was something he'd never voiced aloud. "I love you guys."

"You know he'll come back." Her father sounded both patient and certain. "And you need to talk to him when he does. Georgie, he wasn't with that woman. She was just there. She jumped in and kissed him for the cameras. I'm positive that's the truth." He hunkered down in front of her chair and cupped her cheeks. "You know I love you, right?" At her nod, he continued. "Don't be stubborn like your old dad, Georgie. Don't let your pride stop you from having the love of a lifetime."

Georgie pulled her shoulders up to her ears and hunched deeper into the chair. "It's not like that. He doesn't love me. I can't stand in his way. He's going to be the president. I… His father's right. I wouldn't be a good first lady." Tears gathered on her lashes and she dashed them away with the back of her hand. "I can't face him, Daddy. There's no magic wand to wave to make it all better."

"When did you stop believing in magic, baby girl?"

"When the shadows got so dark I couldn't see any longer."

"Aw, honey."

"Don't, Dad. Just…don't. The doctors say a fifty-fifty chance." A bittersweet smile formed on her face. "Today I feel half-dead."

"Don't say that, Georgeanne. Don't you give up." Her father pushed to his feet and stomped over to stare out the window. "Dang it. I hate this. I hate seein' you weak and pale. You were never sick as a kid. You'd be out there even when the winter wind was cold enough to steal your breath. I'd be out there workin', look up and there you'd be on top of ol' Lucky, movin' the cows to shelter."

He glanced at her over his shoulder. "I remember one time in particular. You came runnin' in the house, your cheeks as red as apples, laughin' and hidin' a snowball behind your back. What happened to that little girl?"

"She grew up, Daddy. Grew up and went away. Do you still love what she left behind?"

"That's a hellava thing to ask me, girl! Of course I love you. I'm your father. No matter what." He grabbed a pillow and punched it a couple of times before gently easing it behind Georgie's back. "Now, you listen to me, baby girl. You're gonna win this fight. And if you had a lick of sense in that way too smart head of yours, you'd call Clayton Barron and tell him to get his ass down here."

"No." Georgie pulled her sweater a little tighter around her shoulders. She was always cold these days. Her chair faced the window. She could see the lake where she'd learned to fish and had gone swimming with her horse on hot summer days. The afternoon sun flared just above the horizon, teasing the water with glittering fingers.

This was why she'd come home. Not to die, but to heal, surrounded by the place that *made* her. She was so scared these days. Afraid of saying goodbye to those she loved. Afraid of living the moments she had left. The look on Clay's face when she'd told him echoed in her dreams, a ghost she could neither touch nor exorcise.

Her dad dropped a kiss on her head. "Rest, baby girl. I love you."

Georgie called after him, her voice just loud enough to be heard over the clomping of his boots. "I love you, too, Daddy."

The glinting path of sunlight pulled her into the dream—the one she always reached for when the pain from the treatments got too bad.

The sun, sinking in the sky, spilled in the window and drenched Clay in shimmering gold. The light made a halo around him she knew he deserved, and he looked incredibly right mantled in the splendor. He was Oklahoma's favorite son, would be president one day soon. She admired him from afar, knowing she could never touch him, never share in the warmth of his golden glow. As she turned to walk away, he called her. And then she was in his sheltering arms, warm and safe. He dipped his head, his firm lips finding hers. She sighed, offering everything she had, everything she was, to him.

The wooden floor creaked and she startled awake. So she thought. A waking dream stood in front of her. Clay, bathed in the copper light of the setting sun. She blinked, then rubbed her eyes.

"I've missed you, sweet pea."

"Why are you here?" She shaded her eyes against the glare. Clay stood there handsome and…perfect.

Clay squatted in front of her. "I'm here because you are, Georgie."

"But…the campaign—"

"Can take place without me for a while."

"You don't mean that."

"Don't put words in my mouth, Georgie. You quit that job, remember?"

She was shocked for a moment, but caught the hint of a smile teasing the side of his mouth. Without considering the consequences, she touched his lips.

When he spoke, his breath teased her fingers. "I'm an idiot and a fool, Georgie. Can you forgive me? I've missed you more than words can say." Clay leaned closer, brushed his lips against hers. "And I love you more than life."

Unsure she'd heard correctly, she demanded, "Say that again."

"I love you, Georgie. Please forgive me. Please love me back. I won't fail you again."

"Is that a campaign promise, Senator?" Her voice was haughty and sarcastic.

"No, Georgeanne Dreyfus, that's a promise from my heart."

Twenty

Clay stayed with Georgie on the ranch, working toward redemption. He took her horseback riding when she felt strong enough. He held her cuddled on his lap in the big chair facing the wide window when she didn't. He kept her warm when her body shook with chills. He kissed her bald head and told her she was more beautiful than that Irish singer from the '80s who'd shaved her head. He told her he loved her. Every chance he got.

He talked to her, using his words, not hers. He opened his heart to her, whispering plans for the future—*their* future. He didn't mention surgery. The decision was hers. He did his best to give her hope and love, and a reason to stay with him. And he bought a ring. On a day between treatments when her color was better, when she held down breakfast, when her eyes weren't dulled with pain, he led her outside to a saddled horse.

Clay mounted, maneuvered to the edge of the porch and pulled her across the saddle in front of him. At a slow walk, they rode out and, after a short circuit of her dad's ranch, Clay guided the horse to the swath of lush grass near the lake. A picnic was set out there, arranged with the help of Cassie and Jolie, who snuck in after he and Georgie left the house. Dismounting carefully, he reached up and gathered her into a princess carry and strode to the blanket stretched across the grass.

The sun edged toward the horizon, the light soft as sunset approached. He offered her cold watermelon. He offered her cheese and crackers. He opened and poured two crystal flutes of sparkling grape juice. Then he positioned himself on one knee and took her hand.

"You know I love you, yeah?" He watched her expression, searching for a flicker of doubt. There was none when she answered.

"Yes. I know. And you know I love you, right?"

Finding he could breathe again, he nodded. "Right." He leaned forward and kissed her, a chaste brush of his lips across hers. They hadn't had sex in weeks and he didn't care. She was too fragile and that was okay. Holding her, sleeping with her in his arms, was even more satisfying than the bells and whistles of climaxes. He finally understood love, understood "for better or worse, in sickness and in health."

She sat with her back to the lake, and the sun kissed the treetops on the other side, even as it painted a gilded path across the water. Georgie was bathed in a golden aura and she'd never looked more beautiful. Holding her hand, he reached into the picnic basket and retrieved a box. With a move he'd practiced until it was flawless, he opened the jewelry box with one hand and hooked the one-carat, emerald-cut diamond solitaire with his index finger.

"I'm not waiting any longer. I want to spend the rest of our lives together. Georgeanne Ruth Dreyfus, will you marry me?"

Georgie stared, tears glittering like the sun dancing on the placid water behind her. She whispered one word and the breath he'd been holding rushed out.

"Yes."

He gathered her into his arms, kissed her with gentle lips that turned demanding, his tongue seeking hers, his hands careful, but clear in their declaration of how much he desired her.

"Thank you, sweet pea."

Clay didn't leave her often, but his numbers were falling. She fretted. Georgie believed in him, was convinced he'd be the next president. And she forced him back on the campaign trail with an argument—started by her—that left her exhausted. He didn't like being apart, scared he was missing minutes and seconds with her that he'd never get back. He shared those fears with Cord and Chance, with Boone and Hunt. He lay awake, terrified he'd get a call saying he'd missed it all.

He argued with the old man. He brooded. And he replayed Georgie's parting words over and over.

Don't you get it? This is bigger than me. Than you. Than us. This is the whole country, Clay. They need you. You can fix it. You can make it better just like you fixed my heart and made me whole.

So here he was in St. Louis, staring at his reflection in a makeup mirror. Georgie's words weren't the only ones he heard.

When it comes time for the acceptance speech at the party's convention, it better be you givin' it, boy.

His father's words remained scorched in his memory. The makeup girl babbled about his perfect hair, perfect face, perfect everything, until he wanted to growl and jerk away. He didn't need to look at the text on his phone, that message also seared into his psyche. Leave it to his sister-in-law to get right to the point.

The girl reached to comb his hair and he snagged her wrist. "Enough. You're done." She sputtered, but left him alone in the dressing room. Unable to help himself, he reread Cassie's text.

Georgie scheduled for surgery tomorrow morning. It better be you sitting beside her bed when she wakes up.

Surgery. He knew what that meant. Chemo and radiation had failed. The doctor had finally talked sense into Georgie. But she hadn't told him. He swallowed the anger. Georgie should have told him. He knew what she was doing—trying to protect him, protect the campaign. But she should have told him to come because nothing was more important than her.

Dammit, this was the last-ditch effort to save Georgie's life. She'd all but shoved him away, refused to talk to him about her treatment. Not that he could blame her. After what his old man said about her, knowing about his own experience with his mother, she had every right to be skittish, despite the fact she wore his engagement ring.

He had a speech to give—an important speech that would make or break him before the convention. But his heart wasn't in it. His heart wasn't even in the same building. It was with the woman he loved who was facing surgery without him because she was protecting his damn political career.

Clay stared out over the sea of faces, those beyond the first few rows nothing but blurry smudges in the darkened auditorium. Out of habit, he glanced into the wings but the figure he sought was no longer there because she was alone in Oklahoma facing a life-changing event. Inhaling, he continued the speech, saying the words Georgie had written for him.

"I met a man the other day, a man who served this country in three wars, a man who wasn't shy about his opinion. 'You know what I think, son?' he asked. 'No, sir, but I'd like to,' I replied. 'I'll tell ya what's wrong with the government. It's politicians. We got too many of 'em. We don't need any more of them durn politicians. What we need is more legislators. Folks who understand why they've got them fancy desks up there in the Capitol. We need smart folks workin' for the people. Not the people working for all them politicians. Here's the thing, son. Us folks out here in the vast middle of the country? We ain't got time for jawin' and fancy words. We're plain-speakin'. You gotta say what you mean and mean what you say—'"

Clay glanced down at the cards on the podium. He never used a teleprompter when Georgie wrote his speeches, as she had this one, but those last words struck him dumb. Damn but he missed her. He stared out across the audience and then glanced once more to the wings of the stage. No shadowy figure stood there mouthing the words with him. No Georgie. And there might not be a Georgie after tomorrow.

He had to breathe around the ache in his chest and he realized he'd been silent long enough that the crowd was growing restless. Clearing his throat to swallow the lump that had formed there, he continued.

"Some time ago, someone important to me was faced with a decision. She didn't consult me. She didn't ask my opinion. She made a choice and when I found out, her decision was one I didn't like. Now it's my turn to make a decision. It might be one she doesn't like, but it's the right one for me. For her. For us."

Furtive activity at the edge of the stage drew his attention. Boone stood there, hands shoved in his front pockets, watching with a slightly twisted grin on his face. It was the man and woman—the hacks hired by Cyrus to replace Georgie—who were waving frantically to get his attention. He ignored them and turned back to the audience.

"Thank you for coming and good night." Clay swiveled on his heel and headed for Boone. By the time he'd crossed the stage, Hunt was standing there, as well.

"Where to, boss?"

Clay studied his security chief for a long moment. "Where is she?"

Hunt deferred to his brother. Boone tucked his chin in a short nod of approval as he answered, "OU Med. They checked her in tonight."

"Then that's where we're going."

Thing One and Thing Two swarmed him.

"You can't!" From her.

"You didn't finish that travesty of a speech." From him.

Clay almost laughed when Hunt caught his left elbow and Boone snagged his right arm and blocked the two from reaching him. Hunt had his phone up to his ear issuing quiet orders into it. One of the organizers came puffing up.

"Senator Barron? Is there a problem, sir?" The man wasn't quite wringing his hands, unlike the Twit Twins.

"A family emergency."

"Oh. Oh! Your fiancée. Of course. I'm sorry. Is there anything I can do?"

Get out of my way for starters, Clay thought. Rather than voicing it, he smiled but kept walking. "We have it under control, thank you. Perhaps you could draft someone to fill the rest of the time set aside for my keynote?"

"Oh! Yes, yes, of course. I should do that." The man peeled away and huffed back the way they'd come.

As they reached the SUV idling at the side entrance, Clay turned to the two handlers. They'd fussed and dive-bombed him like mockingbirds with a cat in sight of their nest the whole way. "I've wanted to say this since the day you first appeared in my office. You're fired."

Clay, wearing exhaustion like a wrinkled suit, sat next to the hospital bed watching the woman he loved beyond reason. Her skin, paper-thin and translucent, felt like dry silk beneath the one finger he used to caress her arm. Georgie opened her eyes and when they widened in sleepy surprise, he smiled.

"Hello, sweet pea."

"Clay?"

"Yeah?"

"Are you really here?"

"Oh, yeah, love. I'm really here. Not going anywhere."

"But…you can't be here."

His brow knit as he stared at her. "I'm here. There's no *can't* about it."

"But…your speech."

"Given."

"You're supposed to be on your way to Denver."

"Nope. I'm supposed to be right here."

"Clay!"

"Georgie."

Color suffused her pale cheeks and the readout of her blood pressure on the machine next to her bed spiked.

"The campaign!"

"Is over."

Her mouth gaped open. She closed it. It gaped again. She breathed a shocked question. "What?"

"I'm done."

"But the polls—"

"Don't mean jack." He carefully took her hand. "I'm out, Georgie. I'm not running."

She blinked, eyes going wide. "You can't do that."

"I can and did."

"But—"

"Shush, Georgie."

"But—"

He leaned in and kissed her before she could finish speaking. He spoke against her lips. "No buts. Just listen, okay?"

When she nodded and whispered, "Okay," he straightened. "You've always been my heart, Georgie. And your words? Your words make me want to be the man you think I am. I haven't been that man lately, but I'm going to be."

"Clay—"

"Shhh. I'm talking, sweet pea." He lifted the hand he was holding and brought it to his lips for a kiss. "As president, I have eight years. *Only* eight years. I can do a lot of good, but the next person who steps in behind me can undo everything I've put into place."

He paused, gathering his thoughts. "Your words last night, they hit home and made sense. Do you remember the words you gave me to say?"

Her expression morphed into one of confusion so he quoted the words back to her. "I'll tell ya what's wrong with the government. It's politicians. We got too many of 'em. We don't need any more of them durn politicians. What we need is more legislators. Folks who understand why they've got them fancy desks up there in the Capitol. We need smart folks workin' for the people. Not the people working for all them politicians. Remember now?"

At her nod, he continued. "You're right. I don't want to be a politician. I want to be a legislator. I can't do that as president. I can by staying in the Senate. So that's what I'm doing—staying in the Senate."

His thumb brushed the tear trickling down her cheek before he kissed her. "I love you, Georgie Dreyfus, with everything I have. With everything I am. I want to make you proud."

"You do. Every day of my life, Clayton Barron. You do."

Georgie was coming home today. Clay could barely contain himself. He hated hospitals. Hated the sounds and the smells and sadness that permeated the very air. He waited outside her room while a nurse performed a final check of Georgie's vitals and changed bandages. He'd already participated in that routine, and had been schooled in all things aftercare.

Finished, the nurse slipped out, offering him a smile and an arm squeeze as she passed. "Take care of our girl," she murmured.

"Always."

He walked into the room. Georgie couldn't get dressed until the final consult with the surgeon. Jolie had packed clothes for her, but Clay had his own ideas. He set the box he'd brought in her lap as he bent to kiss her.

"Can't wait to have you home, sweet pea."

Georgie stared at the box before raising her eyes to his.

"Open it, love."

Her fingers trembled, rustling the tissue paper filling the gold-foil box. Her throat worked, contracting as she swallowed. Her gaze barely lingered after colliding with his.

Clay attempted to speak, but the words came out mangled, his voice a rusty saw on metal pipe. He cleared his throat, spoke again. "Georgie? What's wrong?" His insides twisted as he second-guessed the gift. Maybe it was too soon. Or too much. Or maybe he was the world's biggest idiot. "Sweet pea?"

Her fingers again fussed with the tissue, her shoulders slumping as her chin tucked against her chest. "Why did you buy this?"

Her question was whispered from between chapped lips, and he was torn between kissing her or passing her the water glass with the bent straw. "Because I wanted you to have it."

"But it's red lingerie." She looked up, her eyes holding some emotion he wasn't sure he wanted to identify.

"You were wearing red lingerie in my bathroom in Scottsdale. And you wore red lingerie the first time we made love." He cupped her cheek in his hand. "Red is your color."

Her tears caught Clay by surprise. He settled next to her on the hospital bed, gathering her close. Brushing them away with a gentle swipe of his thumb, he kissed her forehead. "You're beautiful, Georgie, and I love seeing you in sexy lingerie."

She pushed against him ineffectually and the scarf on

her bald head slipped off. “No, I’m not. I’m not beautiful. I’m not sexy.”

“Look at me, sweet pea. You will always be beautiful to me because I love you.”

“Even sick?” She flicked a hand toward her bandaged chest. “Even without these?”

“You’re alive. That’s all that matters.” He kissed her then, deep and sweet, to prove his point. That she was alive and that he loved her. Always.

Epilogue

Georgie floated down the gentle slope on her father's arm. Clay waited for her at the base of the golden path across the placid lake that led to the setting sun. His family waited with him—his cousin Boone and his brothers Cord, Chance, Chase and Cash. His nephew CJ, clutching a satin pillow with their wedding bands tied to it, stood on his right. Opposite them, her best friend and maid of honor, Jen, and her soon-to-be sisters Cassie and Jolie smiled at her.

Clay's father was notably absent. Her mother was notably not, standing on the left in her designer mother-of-the-bride dress. Ev and her husband were there, as were other friends, including Miriam Davis, the reporter from the *Washington Post*. The Tate brothers surrounded their mother. Deacon Tate stood at the back of the congregation, strumming an acoustic guitar, the song soft and romantic and perfect.

Clay stepped forward to meet her, accepted her hand when her father took it from the crook of his arm as he kissed her cheek. "I love you, baby," her dad murmured. "Take care of my little girl, Clayton."

"Always." No hesitation. No regret. The word filled with the promise of the rest of their lives. The news from her doctor, received that morning, guaranteed the future. Cancer-free. Follow-ups, but she was clear of the disease.

The ceremony was traditional. Clay's eyes were warm and moist as he said the words, "For better, for worse, in sickness and in health, to love and to cherish until death do us part."

She added her own promise to his.

When the minister pronounced them man and wife, Clay kissed her, deeply, thoroughly and with tongue before scooping her into his arms, still kissing her, much to the amusement of their audience. He didn't put her down but carried her up the hill to the backyard of her dad's house. The caterers had been busy.

Photographs. Hugs. Kisses. Well-wishes. Toasts. Cake. More toasts. And then she was in Clay's arms as Deacon and the Sons of Nashville sang Clint Black's "When I Said I Do" for their first dance. Clay held her close and moved with the music while she let the words wash over her. This wasn't the song she'd picked, but it was perfect.

Clay twirled her out and reeled her in only to bend her into a dip. He kissed her arched throat and whispered, "Are you wearing it?"

She blushed but nodded, thinking about the bridal tradition. She wore her grandmother's pearls for her something old. The blue satin ribbon garter on her right thigh got the color right. She even had a real sixpence in one of the white cowgirl boots she'd borrowed from Cassie. Clay, however, was not referring to any of those things.

"Yes," she sighed before her breath caught at the sexy glints in his eyes. Clay owned her heart.

Beneath the silk organza and lace of her full-skirted wedding gown, she wore a red satin bustier and panties—the same lingerie he'd gifted her with that day in the hospital. She hadn't worn the ensemble until she slipped into it that afternoon as she dressed for their wedding. She'd saved it for the moment he'd hold her in his arms, when he kissed her and made love to her for the first time as man and wife. This was her something new—the promise of the new life he'd given her there in her hospital room.

"Good," he murmured against her lips. "Red is definitely your color."

* * * * *

If you loved this novel,
pick up all the books in the
RED DIRT ROYALTY *series*
from Silver James

COWGIRLS DON'T CRY
THE COWGIRL'S LITTLE SECRET

And pick up these other sexy and emotional
Western reads from Harlequin Desire

TWINS FOR THE TEXAN
by USA TODAY *bestselling author Charlene Sands*

TAKE ME, COWBOY
by USA TODAY *bestselling author Maisey Yates*

THE RANCHER'S MARRIAGE PACT
by Kristi Gold

Only from Harlequin Desire!

***

If you're on Twitter, tell us what you think
of Harlequin Desire! #harlequindesire